the
Name
Tree

also by

ANTHONY WOOD

A Tale of Two Colors

White & Black

Gray & Blue

Peace Before the Second Storm

The Storm That Carries Me Home

The Fire That Calms the Storm

Storm of Terror

Nonfiction

Up Close & Personal: Embracing the Poor

the Name Tree

HE HAD TO LOSE HIS DAUGHTER TO SAVE HER.
AND HIMSELF.

ANTHONY WOOD

OTTERFORD
BENTONVILLE, ARKANSAS

OTTERFORD

An Imprint of Roan & Weatherford Publishing Associates, LLC
Bentonville, Arkansas
www.roanweatherford.com

Library of Congress Cataloging-in-Publication Data
Names: Wood, Anthony author.
Title: The Name Tree
Description: First Edition | Bentonville: Otterford. 2024.
Identifiers: LCCN: 2024946560 | ISBN: 978-1-63373-996-3 (hardcover) |
ISBN: 978-1-63373-997-0 (trade paperback) | ISBN: 978-1-63373-998-7 (eBook)
Subjects: | BISAC: FAMILY & RELATIONSHIPS/Death, Grief, Bereavement |
SELF-HELP/Death, Grief, Bereavement |
BODY, MIND & SPIRIT/Afterlife & Reincarnation
LC record available at: https://lccn.loc.gov/2024946560

Otterford trade paperback edition March, 2025

Cover Design by Casey W. Cowan
Interior Design by Staci Troilo
Editing by Staci Troilo, Lisa Wood & Lisa Lindsey

DEDICATION

For Naomi. I will find you on the other side.

FOREWORD

"The spirit is willing but the flesh is weak." —Matthew 26:41

I know a little something about weak flesh. We all do. What you're going to find in the following pages is different. It's the story of weak spirit. Two spirits, actually. Mine, and also my daughter's. I'm here to tell that tale.

My daughter isn't.

If you've suffered the loss of a family member due to suicide, you can empathize with my abject, unending grief. And if you considered joining that loved one in the afterlife, you understand where I'm coming from. Maybe it's not fair to call it a weakness of spirit. Perhaps it's more appropriate to label it a void. A vacuum where spirit once was.

When my daughter died, I didn't have the tools to process my loss. Or if I did, I didn't have the ability to apply them to my situation. I was completely hollowed out, and nothing but my child could fill the ever-growing hole inside me. It expanded exponentially until it devoured me, a gaping maw that chomped and chewed until there was nothing left. I succumbed to the vast swelling emptiness and surrendered my life. I wished it away. I prayed for it to end. And when those tactics failed to work, I took matters literally into my own hands.

I'm only able to share my story because my daughter—my dear, sweet, departed daughter—saved me.

This is not a how-to manual. This isn't a checklist of steps for you to complete to heal from your mourning. In fact, I absolutely do not recommend you follow my path. But I want to share my experience in the hope that you find a way through your own darkness to live in the light again.

I am not a licensed therapist. I am not offering a diagnosis or treatment protocol, nor do I advocate you suffer on your own. If you need help, seek it. No, do more than that. Find it, immerse yourself in it. Embrace the knowledge and experience a professional employs to make your recovery faster and fuller than you can imagine.

This "story" (I hesitate to use the word because this isn't fiction) is not really mine. I firmly believe when I sat down to write this, my daughter's message flowed through me. That's why I say we're co-authors. I may have done the typing, but the following pages are her words pouring forth into my heart and into this document. It's not organized the way I would have ordered it had I written it on my own, and it doesn't even sound like my voice, which are two of the many ways I know I didn't "write" this. No, I felt her—channeled her—every step of the way. But I couldn't bring myself to change it to sound like me. This is Naomi's last message to the world, and though it's her version of my story, I agree with her take on all of it.

I—no, WE—hope this book is proof to you that there is a way through the pain. Especially knowing you and your loved one will see each other again. We just don't want you to make that day come sooner than it needs to.

We appreciate you taking a chance on our story and wish you peace and healing.

— Anthony and Naomi

We have been called to heal wounds,
to unite what has fallen apart, and to
bring home those who have lost their way.

—St. Francis of Assisi

Soul, Know Thyself

Until knowledge weds experience, wisdom cannot exist. Discovering
oneself to be unaware opens the door to acceptance. Acceptance seeks
understanding. Understanding desires knowledge. Knowledge sifts
experience. Experience keeps knowledge honest.

Wisdom is the faint glimmer of gold found under a rock in the rushing
stream of life. When books written by others are the sole undergirding
of wisdom, one has yet to explore her own soul. When experiential
knowledge found in the depths of the inner person eclipses books and
theory, the soul will change, grow, and heal.
Only then will the True Person within
stand and take her first step on a new path of light.
Thus, self-reflection is a key sign of wisdom.

—the author, March 15

There is a light, if only we're brave enough to see it.
If we're only brave enough to be it.

—Amanda Gorman

I know the difference between a person good and bad. I've been both.

—the author, March 15

PROLOGUE

Not until we are lost do we begin to understand ourselves.

—Henry David Thoreau

I LEANED AGAINST the old beech tree where Naomi and I once carved her name into the smooth gray bark, pills in one hand, whiskey bottle in the other.

I refused to believe Creator would ever give up on Naomi. Or me. Not possible. After all, was it not Creator who made us? From Himself? How could He abandon Himself?

There was no other way but this. If my reasoning was flawed, so be it. I decided that I would just have to live with it. Rather, die with it.

I didn't want to die, but I couldn't live. Not with Naomi gone.

I had to find my daughter, even if it killed me.

I had no one to turn to. Except Creator.

There are better things ahead than any we leave behind.

—C.S. Lewis

PART ONE

March 15
The First Anniversary of
Naomi's passing.

Death is but a profound invitation to continue the story.

—*the author*

CHAPTER 1

Not an Anniversary to Celebrate

The thing I must do is beyond my understanding.

—the author

MARCH 15. A date I'll never forget. It's the first anniversary of my daughter's death.

4:15 a.m.

I had been wide awake staring at my laptop for two hours, nursing a cold cup of coffee. I wanted to go back to sleep and stay there forever. But I couldn't.

A thousand distinguishable thoughts raced through my head, scattering in every direction like so many multicolored confetti ribbons in a New York City parade. But this parade offered no celebration, like when World War II ended or man walked on the moon for the first time.

Only grief.

The dust devil swirling around in my head stopped with a start. The ribbons fell into a meaningless heap. My mind empty, my remaining bit of reasoning gathered around a single thought. What I wanted to do wasn't what I should do. Not according to conventional wisdom—whatever that was. Contrasting emotions tossed my heart this way and that—brave and afraid, determined and conflicted, spinning my heart like a child's toy top, all at the same time.

Just an hour earlier, I tried to write a letter before I exited, but words were as elusive as dry leaves shooed away by a fall breeze on winter's approach. I wrapped myself in my old sweater to ward off the cold that early spring morning then, hoping it would help, stumbled into the kitchen to reheat my coffee in the microwave. My preference was strong Colombian that day, softened with almond milk and sweetened with a hint of fine Scotch whiskey, the caffeine to wake me, the Scotch to soothe my nerves.

Neither worked.

Though fully awake, I couldn't be consoled. I wouldn't allow it. Relief was not mine to command into the dark crevices of my grieving soul. I threw off all comfort, which would only weaken my resolve. Why my daughter decided to take her life had shaken me awake every night for a year to the same conclusion.

It's hard to face what I've been asked to do by none other than my own soul.

I was a failed father who wanted to help his lost and estranged daughter find herself. I wanted redemption before she took her life, to make things right between us. That didn't happen. No story book ending. Only loss. Devastation. Grief. In no easy terms, that's the deal.

Naomi was gone.

I had to find her.

No matter the cost.

Even if I had to die.

If I had to sacrifice my soul.

I wrote the letter—the farewell letter—to my wife. One Naomi didn't write to me.

Love is not affectionate feeling, but a steady wish for the loved person's ultimate good as far as it can be obtained.

—C.S. Lewis

CHAPTER 2

No Misconceptions Here

The visible world is an active doorway to the invisible world,
and the invisible world is much larger than the visible.

—Richard Rohr

MUG IN HAND, I left my laptop to make a fresh cup of coffee, an unnecessary task undertaken merely to avoid looking at the letter to my wife again. My mind drifted back to my childhood as a night bird sang her mournful dirge. I listened for a long time. Old memories offered a bit of hope.

While growing up, I never had to decide if the things that go bump in the night were real or not. I'd been seeing those who made the noises since childhood. Even then, the unseen was as real to me as the seen. I wasn't afraid of what I witnessed, fear simply being the inability or the lack of desire to face the unknown. Nothing was to be left unknown to me. If it was, I stepped toward it, not away from it.

To find Naomi, I had to step forward into the greatest unknown I would ever come to know. Thankfully, I received a bit of preparation for what would happen soon.

My great-grandmother, whom we called Granny, was a mystic. She taught me about the thin veil separating the seen from the unseen. Granny often said, "Death is just a door between worlds that can be wandered in and out of effortlessly if you but still your soul."

Early on, I realized I possessed a knack for finding the thin spots, as the ancients once called them. Those special places where the barrier between the seen and unseen blurs, and the presence of those long since passed can be seen, felt, and understood. Or maybe it's more accurate to say the thin spots drew me to them. I learned to sit still in silence and solitude for long periods of time, listening and sensing. The wisdom of mystics and spiritual guides of the centuries and from around the world captured my young mind and helped me understand what most choose to dismiss in their narrow and reasoned way of thinking—that what we see with eyes of flesh is not everything.

My journey would take me beyond earthly limitations.

The coffee in my hand had grown cold once more. As cold as my soul. Both needed warming up. A microwave and memories helped. Until my mind took me back to that day.

The day Naomi took her life.

Compassion is the keen awareness of the interdependence
of all things.

—Thomas Merton

CHAPTER 3

One Year Ago

Grief only exists where love lived first.

—Franchesca Cox

THE MORNING AFTER my daughter took her life, my heart weighed heavy as a ship anchor on its way to the bottom of the sea. The increasing pressure as I sank into the deep forced me to think about things I'd carefully tucked away in cavernous places within. Only I knew their location. Only I had the key to the carefully guarded gate of my soul. If I didn't exhale the unmistakable truth I knew as real, I'd never surface. And as I sank to the bottom of my spiritual ocean, my soul would be crushed like an egg.

Landing on the seabed of my dark spirituality gave light to begin my quest to find Naomi. Yet the bottom was quite unsettling. I had nowhere to turn but to those who had walked the less traveled path. How could I have known it would test the very limits of my existence? Even mystics draw a line in the sand for how much help they can give. As one wrote, "The experience is yours. Go alone, and all goes with you." I was alone but willing to go.

My first step would be to revisit the tree where I'd carved Naomi's name when she was but eleven years old. It stood in a nearby state park forest, where she and I had once roamed hills and gullies. A friend told me my journey to find Naomi would begin at the tree. Naomi and I would meet there. Uneasy, my hesitation was not about encountering spirits in the unseen. I'd met other beings and spirits a number of times in both expected and unexpected places. My concern was whether Naomi would want to see me.

The police had found Naomi in the bathroom on a Friday evening. Later, the investigator told me she had left me no farewell letter as she did others. I wanted to scream, "Why?"

A friend tried to console me with the theory that Naomi gave the others what they needed to go on with life because that's where their relationship with her ended—in the seen—whereas I didn't need one because Naomi knew I would come for her. That didn't make much sense then.

So, I set out to find the Name Tree.

I had misgivings about visiting the tree and even rescheduled the trip a couple of times. Finally, I found the courage to call the park office three days before I planned to go. A ranger said the gates would be open the day I was called to visit. Though he gave my body permission, a familiar voice from my past—unmistakably Granny—called my soul to go.

A heavy blanket of depression engulfed my heart throughout the entire early Sunday morning drive. Something wasn't quite right, but I couldn't put my finger on it.

I arrived at a locked gate to find "No Trespassing" signs, threats of prosecution, and yellow caution tape stretched in all directions. My disappointment swelled. Due to a worldwide pandemic, new restrictions had been put into place the day before I arrived—one day—blocking my path to search for the Name Tree and maybe meet Naomi. Disoriented and hurt, I cried.

I stood at the gate for a long time, not knowing what to do. Had I done something wrong? Was it not the right time? Did my daughter not want to see me? From the ridge road on which I parked, I sensed Naomi's presence somewhere deep in the hollows below. My soul burned to find her, to race into the forest, find her, and hold her. I considered breaking the law, but that would have only caused more harm—to me, but more so to her. I would have gladly camped at the gate until the governor lifted the park restrictions, but that would only worry my wife and possibly put a stop to my mission before it fully started.

Gates. Damned things kept worlds, and people, apart.

Wearily, I returned to my truck. When the park reopens, I'll be right here waiting for the damn gate to open. I'll find the tree and start my quest there.

I finally accepted that for some unknown reason, it was not the right time to visit the tree that day. Maybe I just wasn't ready. Maybe Naomi wasn't. I made the two-and-a-half-hour drive back home in five hours.

I cried most of the way.

A COLD SHIVER snaked down my spine to wake me from thoughts of that visit as I stared at my laptop. Sipping coffee that had become cold again, it came to me. It wasn't just the tree in the forest I needed to rediscover.

I must go to *the* tree to find Naomi. The tree beyond what the eyes can see. The Name Tree.

Everyone sees the unseen in proportion to the clarity of their heart.

—Rumi

PART TWO
Retracing Old Footprints

"Say, Pooh, why aren't you busy?" I said.
"Because it's a nice day," said Pooh.
"Yes, but—"
"Why ruin it?" he said.
"But you could be doing something Important," I said.
"I am," said Pooh.
"Oh? Doing what?"
"Listening," he said.
"Listening to what?"
"To the birds. And that squirrel over there."
"What are they saying?" I asked.
"That it's a nice day," said Pooh.
"But you know that already," I said.
"Yes, but it's always nice to hear that somebody else
thinks so, too," he replied.

—Winnie the Pooh

CHAPTER 4

Our Happiest Day

Happy is the moment we sit together, with two forms,
with two faces, yet one soul. You and I.

—Rumi

It only takes one ray of sunlight through the darkest
cloud to remind us of better times.

—the author

ELEVEN-YEAR-OLD NAOMI SLAMMED the door to my old black-and-gray GMC pickup. She couldn't have known the echoing sound would send every game animal in the dense forest scurrying into the next county. She danced around the end of the truck, putting on her hot pink jacket over her sweatshirt and singing the last lines of "The Way" by the band Fastball. Our squirrel hunt ended before we ever started.

She checked her hair and straightened her clothes. "Okay. I'm ready, Dad."

Naomi wanted to bag her first squirrel, but that wasn't going to happen. And I wasn't convinced I wanted it to. Doing so marked the end of a kind of innocence, and I wasn't ready for her to make that change. Besides, I was pretty sure she wouldn't be so ready to take the life of a small animal once she saw it playing in a tree.

I think she just wanted to connect with how I grew up more than anything else. A sub-rural, southern, reformed-racist redneck who could "skin a buck and run a trotline," as the song goes. She wanted to understand that part of me. And other things, as well.

We set out to explore the hills and hollows, doing our best to spy a bushy-tail feasting on acorns or hickory nuts in the canopy overhead. Funny thing, as I loaded my shotgun, I lost all desire to kill anything. I was just happy to be with my daughter.

It was a perfect afternoon. And though we'd walked many trails before, that day was like our first time wandering the woods together. Fall scents permeated the forest as the sun broke through tree branches like a waterfall. As we started down the steep path into the deep hollow, swirls of falling leaves encircled us like tiny tornadoes trying to figure out who we were.

We half-walked, half-slipped down the faint trail leading to the bottom of the deep gully. Rotting leaves covered the broken path, still slick from the previous night's shower. It was like walking on greased glass. More than once, Naomi grabbed for saplings and vines to keep from landing on her backside and sliding to the bottom of the hollow.

We laughed all the way, sometimes skiing down the slope on our boots. The smell of disturbed dirt cast an earthy fragrance reminiscent of a thousand times spent with the Great Soul of Creator in places just like this. When we reached the bottom of the gully, everything felt new and undisturbed. The earth was just beginning to shut down for the coming winter. Tall oaks and hickories reached for clouds that sailed like ships in an ocean of royal blue sky. The trail was littered with dark green ferns, and a few steps in, a whitetail deer leaped across our path. Birds perched on branches above, singing a host of tunes. Despite being surrounded by so much life, we found no squirrel.

A tiny spring trickled erratic notes like those played on the high end of a piano. Its bubbly music captured us for a few minutes as we gazed back up the steep trail, taking in the depth of our descent. The stream sparkled in the patches of sunlight that found their way through red, yellow, and orange leaves falling from towering oak, hickory, and beech trees.

Naomi marveled at the steep sides of the hollow. "We came a long way down, didn't we?"

I scanned the seemingly insurmountable walls towering over two hundred feet. "Yes, we did."

"I almost busted my butt every step."

"Me, too. That's how it is when you need to get to the bottom of things, no pun intended."

Naomi laughed at my corny joke, then asked, "What's a pun?"

I explained the meaning of the word while I looked both directions to see which way we would go. When Naomi took a step, I patted the air for her to wait for a moment. I scanned the trees for a squirrel.

She picked up an old stick and peeled the bark off with her fingernails. Once the bark was stripped clean, she snapped the stick in two.

"Naomi, we must be quiet if we're going to see any squirrels." I was glad she had broken it.

She sat down in the leaves. "Why do we need to be way down here at the bottom?"

"We can see better looking up into the trees rather than down when squirrel hunting."

Naomi measured the steepness of the gully again, and her eyes widened. "What if I got hurt down here and couldn't get out?"

"I'd carry you out on my back if I needed to. You know that."

"I do. But the truck is so far up there. Are you strong enough to haul me out of here?"

Her line of questioning unsettled me. "Absolutely." I hoped the strength of my response would satisfy her curiosity. It didn't.

"How would we get out?"

"By going up. It's the only way out."

"If I got lost out here all by myself and couldn't find my way out, would you come find me?"

"First of all, you wouldn't be out here by yourself. But yes, I'd search until I found you or die trying."

"You would go that far?"

"Yes."

"Even die?"

"Without question."

"Why would you do that, Dad?"

"I am your father, and that's what dads do."

"It is?"

"Yes."

Naomi snapped her head around like someone called her name. She stretched to get a better line of sight like she'd seen something or someone. She locked in on a point and stared down the hollow.

I followed her gaze but saw nothing.

She stood up abruptly, then started walking like she knew exactly where she was going. "We need to go this way, Dad."

I didn't know what was going on but followed her lead. "Watch for snakes!"

Naomi trotted off in typical Saturday morning soccer playing form, leaving me to keep up as best I could.

We stopped at the end of the hollow, where the gully walls faded into the expanse of a plain extending all the way to the Mississippi River. A broad cottonwood valley stretched beyond our sight. The sound of tugboats straining and groaning as they pushed barges upriver broke the stillness and silence of the windless afternoon.

Naomi gazed up into a large tree. She mouthed the words, "This is it."

I thought nothing of it at the time.

"Can we rest here, Dad? My feet hurt."

I searched the area for unwanted slithering lurkers that could do my daughter harm. Satisfied we were safe, I said, "Sure, let's sit on this log."

She had outgrown her hiking boots, and they were too tight. When she removed them to splash her feet in the cool waters of the creek, she winced at the small blisters forming in several places. But Naomi didn't complain. She never liked getting attention for something like that.

Naomi leaned back against the large tree, hands behind her head, hunching her shoulders up around her neck. She kicked her feet in the cool spring water as she studied the wispy white clouds drifting in the sky.

"Look, Dad. There's a rainbow in that one." The entire spectrum was stretched across the thin cloud like a paint brush stroke.

In that moment, I saw eternity in her eyes. Then, she asked an eternal question.

"Dad, why do some people get to have what they need to live, and others don't?"

The question didn't surprise me. It wasn't the first time she'd asked about topics beyond her young years. Even then, I thought Naomi cared too much for people. Sadness crept into her eyes. For some reason, it made me wonder if she was unsure about her purpose in this world. She wanted all people to be treated the same and couldn't understand why that wasn't the case and would never be.

"You've been helping poor people for a while, haven't you, Dad?

"As a vocation, yes, for several years now. But I've always tried to help people who can't help themselves."

"Why do you help the poor, Dad?"

A good question.

"It's the right thing to do."

"No, Dad. Why do you help the poor?"

The right question.

"When I was about your age, I was changing my clothes after prayer meeting one Wednesday night when it hit me like a ton of bricks. It wasn't what the teacher had taught in Bible class or what the preacher spoke about in his devotional talk. I groaned as a thought welled up in me like a fountain. It had to pour itself out."

"What happened?"

"Your grandfather walked in my room, removing his tie, and asked if I was sick. I blurted out like I was puking, 'I'd rather be poor than rich because we need to understand that poor people need our help.' I didn't completely understand what I was saying back then, but for that brief moment, I believe my dad understood me."

Naomi placed her hand on mine. "I understand."

We sat on that ancient log for two hours. Naomi chattered away like the squirrels we were supposed to be hunting. She talked about anything and everything that popped into her head. I just listened, occasionally answering a question she had already answered for herself.

Naomi's feelings about other people too often made her sad. These conversations helped, but she always came back to the same question. Why do things have to be the way they are? She couldn't seem to grasp why the world needed redemption. If we would all just treat each other better, it would be unnecessary. She couldn't, or wouldn't, accept that some people went hungry at night, while others ate sumptuously, all within sight of each other. And though I had seminary degrees and my chosen vocation was ministering to the poor, I had trouble offering any satisfactory answers.

The hurt in her eyes triggered pain in my soul, a common feeling I'd suffered being close with the people I served each day. Funny thing, I'd had the same questions at her age.

Naomi found a little hope in the same conclusion she came to every time she asked the question. "We'll just have to do something about it, then. Won't we, Dad?"

The sun started to set. I figured we had only a couple of hours before darkness caught us."We best get going. We've got a pretty good climb ahead of us."

She looked up into the grand old beech tree commanding this part of the forest. "Can't we stay just a little longer? This is such a good place."

"Okay, just a little longer. We don't want to climb up that slickety ole hill in the dark, do we?"

Her irises matched the color of the sky as she stared into the heavens. The look in her beautiful eyes changed from giggly pre-teen to that of an old soul. I hadn't seen that before and knew it was not meant for me. She turned her palms upward, waiting to receive something, then closed them tightly like she never wanted to let go of the unseen gift she had received. She bonded with Creator in that moment. I recognized the signs, as I'd done the same when I was her age, in a place not so different than this. I didn't ask her anything. I was blessed to be present to witness it.

She returned from her vision with a light shudder. "I like this tree."

"I do, too."

"It makes me feel safe, like I'm supposed to be here."

"Why do you think that?"

She didn't answer. Naomi traced every branch and followed every limb with her index finger in the air all the way down the four-foot-thick trunk to the semi-exposed ancient roots. It was like she was memorizing its every nuance and unique feature.

I put my arm around her shoulder.

She nestled close like a purring kitten. "What kind of tree is this?"

"It's a beech tree."

"Why did it pick this place to live?"

That was an interesting thought.

"Maybe because she likes putting her toes in the cool water like you do." I grabbed a handful of water from the stream and splashed a little on her.

She laughed but quieted quickly, then threw her legs over the log to face the tree behind her. Like a blind person feeling her way in the dark,

Naomi moved her hand along the slight contours and imperfections in the smooth, gray bark.

I took advantage of the moment. "The old folks used to say if you came upon a beech tree in a creek bottom, you'd found rich farm land."

"This is a good tree?"

"Yes, it is, and one of my favorites."

"So, being here makes me a good person?"

"You are a good person, Naomi, simply because Creator made you so."

"Sometimes I feel lost. I don't always know what I'm supposed to be or what I'm supposed to do."

"I know. Me, either."

She smiled weakly. "I'm not sure I'll ever know."

"That's okay." I didn't know what else to say. This wasn't a conversation with me anyway Naomi was conversing with herself. And Creator.

Naomi placed both hands on the beech tree. "I want this to be our place, yours and mine."

I marked the location in my head for a return trip another day. I took a hunting knife from the sheath on my belt. "Okay, then. This will be our special place." I thumbed the edge to determine the blade's sharpness.

Naomi ran her hand across the gray bark like she was slowly cleaning a chalkboard. Her eyes closed as if she was trying to catch whispers from the ancient beech.

"Find the flattest place on the tree, Naomi."

She looked at the knife, then at me as her hand searched the broad trunk.

I touched the blade to the tree and started drawing a line in the smooth, gray bark.

"What are you doing, Dad?"

"I want us to always be able to find our special place again." I carved the first letter.

"Does it hurt the tree?"

"Nah, carving something in the bark will be just a tickle to her skin. I don't think she'll mind too much. Especially since this is your special tree."

I'd carved initials and names into trees many times when I was a kid, but that was over twenty-five years ago. I wasn't sure if I still had the skill, but this day was too important not to try. Soon, the bright blonde wood underneath the bark formed into letters.

"Wow, Dad. Where'd you learn how to do that?" She shivered with excitement like I'd just completed a masterpiece that deserved to be in a museum.

"I figured out how to do it when I was growing up back home."

Naomi placed her finger on the N, and then traced the grooves of each letter like she was finger painting. Then, she rubbed her fingers across her name like a blind person reading Braille. She leaned back to study my work of art.

"It's my name." She spelled the letters, "N-A-O-M-I. What does my name mean?"

"It means 'pleasant' in Hebrew."

"Hmmm, am I?"

"Yeah, well, most of the time," I joked.

"I want to be, Dad. Sometimes I just don't know how."

"Creator will help you, Naomi."

She pondered that for a moment, then popped me on the shoulder and grinned. "I won't forget this place, ever."

"Me, either."

"I'll always remember I have a tree with my name on it." She hugged the trunk like she was being reunited with a long-lost friend, put her cheek against the smooth, gray bark, then whispered words I couldn't hear.

"Can I ask what you said to the tree?"

"I asked her, 'If I ever need a safe place, could I come here?'"

"What did she say back?"

"There were no words, but a warm blanket of peace wrapped around me, like when I crawl up into your lap and you put your arms around me. You make me feel safe, like I could always count on you to come if I was in trouble."

My heart ached for the times I was too tired from work and didn't let her do that. "I'll do better about that, Naomi."

She smiled. "This is now my tree. My friend."

"It is."

"So, if I ever get lost out here, I just need to wait here for you to come find me."

"That's right."

"I'll never forget you did this for me today, Dad."

I didn't know what to say. How could I know how important this was to Naomi? Except that I had one, too. An old oak in the woods near the home where I grew up.

"Can we come back here again sometime and check on my tree?"

"Sure, we'll come at least once a year on your birthday, and more times if you want."

She patted the tree. "I'd like that."

"Then let's declare this our special place. Only you and I can come here. What do you say?"

"Not even my brother?"

"Not even him. You can count on it."

Naomi hopped off the log, backing up until she could take in the enormity of the mighty beech tree that had called her name. I could see the wheels turning in her mind. Her eyes suddenly went blank like she could see beyond the seen.

Naomi blinked twice and declared, "The Name Tree."

"What?"

"That's what I'm calling our special place. The Name Tree."

In that moment, hundreds of monarch butterflies wisped through the hollow to surround us. Naomi giggled like the girl she was, causing my heart to overflow. We simply enjoyed the moment.

I knew then Creator had anchored Naomi to the truth of the universe, like my tree did for me years ago. I didn't ask why she chose it. She would tell me in her own good time, though I was more inclined to believe it had chosen her.

The butterflies danced away as fancifully as they had come. I didn't ask Creator about the butterflies, either. Creator would reveal that in His own good time.

We sat still, enjoying the silence, when a cardinal lit on a limb in front of us.

"Look, Dad, a redbird."

The bird chirped a sweet tune.

"Cool. They say redbirds carry messages to and from people who have died and those still living."

She cocked her head. "Do you believe that?"

"I do. Just speak a word to the east, and they will wing your message to the other side."

"I promise to do that for you if you will do it for me when the time comes, Dad."

"I promise."

We followed the tiny stream back to the trail that would lead us out of the deep hollow. We laughed as I pulled her up one slippery stretch, and she helped me up another. We topped the ridge as the sun sank in the west across the great river, its waters so blue for such a muddy stream.

We made it to the truck as the last vestiges of light disappeared behind the fading horizon. I stopped to savor the moment. Never had there been a day like this one. As much as I wanted to mark where the Name Tree stood, I wanted to mark this memory deep in my soul more. I didn't want it to end. I didn't want to leave.

I opened the door for Naomi, and then trotted around to get in on the driver's side. I handed her a plastic grocery bag with a surprise inside.

She closed her eyes and felt for the gift. She squealed, "My favorite."

"I bought the fattest and juiciest one I could find."

"Pomegranates are the best. Thanks, Dad." Naomi rolled the pomegranate around in her hands, studying how to open it. She broke into the husk and savored each seed coat.

I turned the key and made sure the stick shift was in first gear. As I revved the motor just a bit to ease off the clutch, Naomi put her hand on mine to hold the stick shift in place.

"Can we just sit for a minute?"

"Sure. Are you all right?"

"Yeah, I'm okay." She sat still and silent. "Dad, this was a good day, wasn't it?"

"The best I've ever had with you."

"Let's promise to never forget it, no matter what happens, okay?" She'd never spoken like that before, and I didn't know what to make of it.

Choking through the lump in my throat, I could only manage, "I won't, Naomi. I promise."

Not long after arriving home, I penned a poem with an obvious answer.

I watched you sprout from nothingness
On the first day of spring when you arrived
Budding on the branch of a towering tree, I asked,
Were you always so beautiful in the mind of God?

If there ever comes a day when we can't be together,
keep me in your heart, I'll stay there forever.

—Winnie the Pooh

CHAPTER 5

The Truth about Naomi and Me

As a child I never imagined that all of the real
monsters in the world would be humans.

—Unknown

AOMI AND I were more alike than either of us would have
admitted. That was good for things like exploring wild places,
enjoying music and art, traveling, and helping people. But as
they say, like poles on a magnet repel each other. Our clashes pretty
much resulted from a continuous battle with my stubbornness, a trait of
which she inherited a generous portion.

Over the years, I had developed a way to manage, or maybe just
prolong facing, the generational anger, abuse, and violence I had
experienced growing up. My way of dealing with me was to retreat deep
within to avoid exploding. I wandered forests and rivers, which offered
me more truth about the universe and peace within my soul than
anything I heard or found in a four-walled church building. Getting
away to be with Creator became not only my escape but also my
salvation. It was in the quiet times that I found a clear path to Creator in
the wildest of places.

Once, I attended a church youth rally at the same age Naomi was
when we found the Name Tree. Hundreds of young people attended

from churches all over. A huge banner hung above the speaker platform emblazoned with a red arrow pointing to heaven. The words One Way were printed on it in bold letters. When the first speaker began, I had hoped he'd speak about the kindness and love for all people Jesus had taught. But he railed on and on about the dos and don'ts teenagers better observe. The usual don't drink, don't dance, don't have sex, or else speech that we suffered through regularly in Bible class.

Then, he started in on the hippie movement, a culture and conviction I had come to appreciate. I knew a few hippies and had grown fond of the freedom they expressed and their disdain for anything institutionalized, especially religion.

The speaker shouted as he made his loudest point. "And know this! You can't worship God under a tree!"

I thought, I've been worshiping God under a tree for years now, and I'm only eleven years old. I got up like I needed to visit the restroom but left the convention center and wandered around Vicksburg, returning just in time for the KFC lunch. I realized at that early age that Creator never was meant to be cooped up in four walls of a church house or could be so easily explained away by some mouthy preacher. Neither was my spirituality. The spiritual awakening that day changed my life.

Naomi was a chip off the old block. She loved the outdoors and could find peace in the stillness of a windless forest or in the flames of a warm campfire. One time, she climbed a tree as far up as she could go, and then stretched to touch the sky. When she came back down, she jumped from the lowest limb into my arms and asked, "Daddy, why?"

I had few answers but understood the question. I had asked the same one as a kid.

Earlier, in the same year we found her tree, Naomi braved a short overnight canoe trip with me on the Mississippi River. Back at school on Monday, she told all of her friends how she had crossed the big river in a canoe with her dad.

One of our greatest adventures together came her junior year in college, when she had an opportunity to study at the University of Hawaii in Hilo as an exchange student. When she asked what I thought, I said, "Go!" I had traveled to Alaska on an adventure when I was the same age.

Daughters being daughters, she had money to live on but not enough to travel there. I helped her get a ticket with only one condition—she would let me come for a week-long visit so we could explore the Big Island together. Watching her leave was hard, but seeing her when I arrived a month later more than made up for it.

She took a break from her dorm room to stay with me in a beautiful oceanside resort. Waves lapping at the volcanic rock formations below our deck sang us to sleep each night. It was living in paradise. Our time together? Even better. We circled the island in a rented car to brave the sulfur fumes of Kilauea volcano and swam with giant sea turtles. Our best moment was hiking five miles across a lava bed to the little-known Green Sand Beach that glistened like billions of tiny emeralds against the turquoise-blue ocean.

Back at our car, we rested near a crowd of college students. Some were having difficulty gathering the courage to launch themselves from the fifty-foot cliff into the ocean below.

In typical old school and somewhat redneck fashion, with no warning, I handed Naomi my glasses and said, "Watch this."

Naomi giggled. "Go, Dad!"

I jogged to the edge yelling, "This is how an old man does it!" I'd done this sort of thing many times growing up in Mississippi.

Screams of "Old Dude" along with several colorful metaphors chased after me as I plummeted toward the ocean with arms waving like I was trying to fly. I thought I would never hit the water. Just before I did, I recognized one voice laughing at the top of her lungs.

Naomi.

She screamed, "That's my dad!"

Her joy made the feat all worthwhile.

As much as I sank deep into the ocean that day in Hawaii, Naomi was even more lost then than when she'd left home. She covered her struggle well with laughter, diversions, drinking, and too much makeup, but she was coming apart at the seams. And I was too self-absorbed to recognize it. I had no clue as to the depth of her pain. I thought I knew my daughter well.

I didn't.

That was the last best week I'd ever spend with Naomi. Like when we found the Name Tree.

———————————

The only thing more dangerous than ignorance is arrogance.

—Albert Einstein

CHAPTER 6

A Lost Child

Forgive yourself for not knowing what you didn't know
before you learned it.

—*Maya Angelou*

A LOST CHILD should be able to recognize another lost child. By the time I realized the depth of Naomi's emptiness, we had drifted away from each other.

Naomi was born with the same red hair and green eyes that my Granny had in her younger days. During the pregnancy, we almost lost her at two months, and again several times after that.

Because I'm so grateful for the time I had with her, this is not easy to say.

I've wondered if we thwarted God's purpose by not letting nature take its course.

That's the most difficult thing I've ever thought. I've never said it to anyone lest they judge me a monster or something worse. But I feel it's a legitimate concern. We all contemplate God's plan. The problem is, we only want good outcomes, not necessarily Creator's plan.

Maybe it wasn't Naomi's time to enter this world. Maybe she wasn't ready. Maybe I wasn't ready to be a father. Maybe we were being prepared for her true birth, but modern medical miracles short-circuited Creator's intentions. Those things, I'll never know. To acknowledge any other possibility than the conventionally good often shakes the faith of the shallow. To suggest an alternative explanation is usually quickly judged.

A person is not redeemed by saving the body, but the soul. Naomi needed to be found.

As her body was no longer with us, I had to go where her soul had gone. I had to envision beyond what the eyes could see.

I can't believe I'm writing this.

Though a troubled child, Naomi acted happy as a lark most of the time. She got both traits honestly but never admitted we were very much alike. Sensing, empathic, and caring to a fault, while at the same time risk taking, clownish, and wild. What a recipe for impactful good as well as potential disaster.

Naomi loved school and did well. She studied hard and for years talked about becoming a teacher. At six years old, she hosted singing concerts with all the children in our apartment complex. She taught Bible class for her peers when she was nine, and we spent a month together in Ukraine on a mission trip when she was just eleven. She would complete her school lessons in the morning and serve tea and cookies to every person who came for Bible study in the afternoon.

At fourteen, she and her best friend from the inner city church we planted sang a beautiful spiritual duet for a crowd of over five hundred church leaders attending a conference. She was self-assured and full of passion in those early years, possessing a desire for life like no other person I'd met. But nothing seemed to satisfy a longing neither she nor I understood.

I suspected she, like me in many ways, believed she had been born in the wrong time. She occasionally spoke with me about feeling out of place in this world. But something changed Naomi when she became a teenager. She began absorbing the pain of friends who weren't as pretty as she was. Then, she began questioning her own self-worth and complained that her looks weren't good enough.

Over the next few years, Naomi changed her hair color every other month, caked on enough makeup for three girls, occasionally drank too much, got traffic tickets, and had a number of car wrecks. She even got caught "parking" when the boy she was with backed into a police car trying to sneak out of a dangerous, drug-infested city park.

She seemed to be steadily reaching but didn't know for what.

Caught up in my work to avoid thinking about my own issues, I didn't take the time to understand Naomi. And the gap between us widened with each passing month.

She spiraled downward rapidly, grasping for anything that might salve her spirit. A few months later, I was disappointed to learn she had joined a college sorority. Not that there was anything wrong with joining, but the reason why she joined concerned me. My heart was broken when I saw the group picture of forty girls. It took me three tries to find my daughter in the picture. There she stood, indistinguishable, sporting the same mannequin stance, cut of blonde hair, caked-on makeup, stylish outfits, and plastic smile as her thirty-nine "sisters." I stared into her eyes in the picture, and it was as if I could see all the way down into her soul, hollow and lifeless, like she had no clue as to who she was.

I didn't know my child anymore, and in some ways, I gave up.

I regret that.

Not long after, Naomi married a college fraternity guy she never really loved. He had little ambition and made little progress pursuing a decent job to help support them. Naomi took care of him and defended him to a fault. More of her misguided empathy. A year into the marriage, she told me she had made a huge mistake. But she kept trying to hold the marriage together.

Naomi finished college and landed a good job with a reputable automobile maker. She started a master's degree program and advanced in her work. Things looked promising. But when my wife and I visited her and her husband several months later, Naomi still had the same fake plastic smile and an inexpressible pain in her eyes. She tried to hide it, but I recognized it easily, as I knew that pain firsthand. My heart ached for her.

Naomi continued searching for her elusive identity. And I continued pretending I didn't see what was happening. I turned my attention inward toward my own issues, my own pain, and in so doing, I failed to help her avoid the same path I walked.

Don't get lost in your pain;
know that one day your pain will become your cure.

—Rumi

PART THREE

Making Sense in an Insensible World

---

*Save me from trendy religion
that makes cheap clichés out of timeless truths.*

—Rich Mullins

CHAPTER 7

The Spoiler

As traumatized children we always dreamed that someone would come and save us. We never dreamed that it would be... ourselves, as adults.

—*Alice Little*

THE ONLY WAY I could begin my quest was to end the one I was on and find the elusive answers to my own troubles, so I could help Naomi find hers. To do that, I had to die. I'd never been afraid of pain but never was a fan of it, either. I planned to take the easy way out. A bottle of prescription sleeping pills chased with a bottle of fine Scotch whiskey. As unsettling as this seemed, I did have good reason to do it.

After Naomi passed, I saw glimpses and felt the warmth of an unseen spirit pass by my chair as I watched late night movies when I couldn't sleep. I heard my name spoken more than once when I thought it was my wife calling from the back bedroom. Except it wasn't her voice. Some say you see and hear what you want to. I say one person's hallucination is another's window into the unseen. Mine was the latter.

Sorting out how I had failed Naomi overwhelmed my soul. What could I have done differently? Why didn't I acknowledge her depression and downward spiral, and then do something about it? Memories, good and bad, saturated my mind to the point of exhaustion.

It was because I hadn't been in her life for some time. A daily painful reminder. The desire to hug her just once more was enough to make me leave this world to find her in the next. The longer I waited, the more I saw glimpses of her in the big living room mirror or from the corner of my eye as she passed by in a veil of dim light.

I tried to reason through why Naomi took her life but found no answers. That only made me more determined to find some.

When her birthday came around six months after her death, I sunk into a deep funk of depression for two weeks. I slept most of the day only to wake more tired than when I lay down. Helpless, hopeless, and defeated, I could neither write nor create.

I knew all the clinical reasons for my state of mind. I'd had enough counseling for a room full of people. I had to face the rawness of my daughter's passing. It had broken my heart and scattered my mind. Head pounding, heart heavy, skin burning, I contemplated Naomi's life and death. My spirit wilted, my soul spiraled downward, and my mind became fixated on but one thing—finding Naomi.

I sat at my laptop trying to write, trying to make sense of it all. One recurring question stalked my soul, the one question I wished I could ask her. The answer to that question would be the start of our journey home.

A red cardinal landed and fluttered in front of my window for at least a full minute, then settled in the tree just opposite from where I sat.

A spark of hope burned in my soul. I dared to believe what I espoused and asked the cardinal to please carry my question through the thin veil to my daughter.

What was so terrible, Naomi, that taking your life became the only answer?

The bird chirped a soft melody, fluttered his wings, then flew to the east.

I wasn't sure I'd be happy with her response.

I asked, "What is the answer to the most important question?"
Creator replied, "To never stop asking that question."

—_the author_

CHAPTER 8

Trying to Make Sense of What I Have to Do

We're not just made by God. We are made of God.

—St. Julian of Norwich

WHEN I GOT the news of Naomi's death, I was devastated. But not completely surprised. Probably because of our family history of suicide attempts—besides myself—an aunt, a brother, and a niece. And sadly, I had a cousin who succeeded. Because of family history and my own struggles, I'd learned how to keep any plan I'd begun to form at bay. Naomi didn't.

She hid her decision well. No one suspected her intention. The times I'd considered the same action, my plan was to simply disappear, never to be found. No one would have known what happened except that I was gone. But still, why did Naomi feel suicide was the best answer? The only answer?

I had to come to grips with my own untried beliefs in order to understand hers. Otherwise, I'd be more lost than she would be when I found her. I dismantled conventional reason so I could understand the unreasonable plan I was forming. I discarded useless and trite beliefs that more reasonable spiritual people held dear in attitudes of righteous judgment.

Ancient mystics taught that until a person knew their own soul, they could never really know God. I found this to be true. The only barriers to knowing Creator were ones I had so carefully built for myself. When things went south in my life, I blamed my spiritual inadequacies on bad parenting, inept Sunday school teachers, abusive church leaders, and hollow theologies that left me knowing a lot about Creator, but never knowing Creator personally. And though no one can completely shake the dust of a thousand bad sermons from their feet, I left many a poor teaching behind in search of a richer world of spiritual understanding. I had to. There were no answers for this.

Growing up in a traditional, conservative, fundamentalist Christian environment, one that was often spiritually abusive, offered few opportunities to sort through things I believed deep within. I sensed early on that all things were connected in the universe, spiritual waves ebbing and flowing in and out of all things, animate and inanimate, sentient and not. I was taught that the firstborn of all creation held it all together. With that, I agreed. I'd known Creator's presence from a young age. Even as a child, I'd wondered what would happen if Creator took His eyes off of Creation, even for a second. Would we return to unimaginable imploding chaos? Had Creator taken his eyes off of me? I was in chaos.

But one thing held me together.

I'd often experienced the thin veil between the seen and unseen. I had encountered thin spots where I connected with those who had left this world for a better one.

Granny spoke of such things in her bedtime stories. She sang about preparing for a journey and how she looked forward to her first grand reunion with friends and family on the other side. She'd smile and tell us they called to her in the stillness of the night. I'd heard that same call.

Not long after she married, Naomi called late one night. "There's a purple, man-shaped being glowing in my closet saying things I can't understand." Later, she described similar experiences she'd had through the years and how some beings seemed familiar, though she couldn't say why. She had the same knack for thin spots as me. "What should I do, Dad?"

"Accept what you've been given and try not to make too much of it." That was all I knew to say at the time.

Naomi's spiritual encounters and "rebellious" beliefs led her to investigate other spiritual paths. She searched everywhere except through Him with whom the answer lay, the One Who Lives Within.

Now that she had crossed to the other side, I opened my soul to any possible path to find Naomi. The thin veil seemed thick as a stone wall as I contemplated my next move.

I asked, "Creator, if you made souls from your essence, can a soul ever be lost? If so, then if a soul becomes lost, can it not be found?"

I contemplated, "If a soul is a part of You, then You cannot destroy You." I trusted that Creator never gave up on a soul.

"Can a soul be born out of time? If mental illness, disease, addictions, talents, and even goodness can be passed from one generation to the next, then could not the soul?"

I completely trusted that Creator brought things into being at their appointed times, even if He had to do a restart. Creator often wrestled with restarts throughout time. He did with the Flood, the Incarnation, and it appears Creator will again at the end of the world.

"If a soul was born out of time, could it not be reborn in the right time?"

I trusted Creator never gave up on His created ones, no matter how long and badly they may have lived, or if they had been born out of time. Compassion the size of Creator's Great Soul cried out in me for something entirely different than what I had been taught—that Naomi could be found even still. And be rescued from her unintended life experiences to be reborn into the life always intended for her.

A child born out of time will find it too difficult to secure her true identity and place in a world not hers. Naomi's misunderstood and unappreciated life was wrought with too much pain and struggle to continue. Unable even to find herself in caring for others, Naomi damaged her holistic health to the point of taking her own life. She lost all hope of finding peace. She left this world to the fools who could only offer hollow and useless answers for her decision.

Naomi didn't need salvation. She needed to be freed from a life she did not choose, a life her parents forced upon her. Naomi didn't choose to be saved at the hospital. We chose that for her. But Naomi did choose to return to the One who held both the question and answer of her true identity, and they lay through the thin veil on the other side.

―――――

I'm not lost. I've simply wandered further into the darkness than you care to brave.

―Unknown

CHAPTER 9

An Empath Run Amuck

God will not judge us on our... human success, but on how much we have loved.

—*St. John of the Cross*

I HAVE ALWAYS been, and forever will be, an empath. Taking on the hurt of others grew deeper as I witnessed how my birth family responded to my father's anger, abuse, and violence. He never understood how much he'd been affected by the same—and worse—experiences as a child. His inability to change impacted me terribly.

Once, on the way home from church, Dad raged about a missing wrench. He blamed me, though I hadn't lost the tool. My younger brother had. I refused to rat on him because I didn't want him to receive the punishment I knew was coming. Walking from the car to the door of our house, Dad screamed at me about losing the wrench. His hot breath singed the back of my neck.

Finally, I'd had enough. I turned, planted my feet, and said, "You will no longer blame me for things I did not do!" With my mother and younger brother both watching, Dad front- and back-handed me seven times. Except for my head snapping back and forth, I never moved a muscle.

It never crossed my mind to fight back.

When he finished, I didn't say anything for a moment. Then, I calmly asked, "How long are you gonna do this? 'Cause I can go all night."

He stomped into the house. Not another word was ever spoken about the incident, but the emotional and psychological damage was done. That's been my reward too many times for being an empath. For my willingness to take one for the team with little regard to how it might affect me. Problem was, I had too many teams that I took hits for in those days. Too many experiences like that made me leave home too soon in search of my lost self.

At nineteen, I escaped a hard-lined, narrow-minded, conservative Christian college before they kicked me out. I didn't enroll to get an education. I went to college to get away from home and run wild. I returned to live in my childhood home, but the intensity of what I'd experienced as a child increased. There was no peace living at home, and no opportunity to seek the me I could not find.

So, I wandered.

I went from working on a bridge in Florida and hanging out on topless beaches to outrunning the cops in my hot rod and coming home the prodigal son at two o'clock in the morning. From trying to settle down with a girl I never loved to traveling to the end of the earth working on the Alaskan Pipeline at Prudhoe Bay. Still, I could not find the peace that only could be had in the depths of my inner person. No job was too hard, no pain too great, no climate too hot or cold, no place too far to travel in my search for the purpose and identity I'd lost so early in the abusive home I was born into.

When I landed in Anchorage, Alaska, I was as lost as a goose in a snowstorm.

After a long hug at the airport, my aunt took me by the shoulders and shook me. "I know why you're here. Just know this. You can be anybody you want to be here."

That sounded good to me.

As I unpacked, my aunt told me she had endured similar experiences with her father, my Papaw. I didn't realize how much of a blessing living in her home would be.

My aunt knew I had to leave what was behind to rediscover the true *me* I had lost, that little boy whose identity had not yet been damaged. She knew because she had done the same thing and was as much or more of an empath than me. Living with my aunt was an interesting experience. She also had engaged in self-destructive behaviors before finding the true peace she sought, but her good soul worked to relieve the agony of others, even to her own detriment. I stopped counting the number of stray homeless cats, dogs, and humans she brought home to live in her house. Like her, I'd given so much of myself away that I had little left for me. Being with my aunt deepened my empathic gift but explained nothing. Fortunately, I fell into a group of Christian guys at church who helped me tremendously. Even though they hadn't experienced the same pain I'd suffered, they made life enjoyable.

Not long after arriving in Alaska, I foolishly believed getting married would help my endless pursuit for peace. Faulty thinking at best. Later, I thought having children surely would bring back the joy lost in my own childhood. Not true.

My pain compounded as I absorbed the struggles of others that led to uncharacteristic behaviors harmful to me and those around me. I volunteered for everything church-related I could—prison ministry, children's worship, Bible class teacher. I'd get so depleted in helping others that I'd forget myself. Life ran out of control like a non-stop recycling DVD but with no pause button on the remote. I'd withdraw, become angry, even violent, truly unfit for human interaction.

I justified my poor behaviors in hopes the good work I did to help others would offset my sin. When I returned to my senses each time, I was devastated over the wrongs I'd done. Self-medication and withdrawal became the answer to numb my lack of understanding.

I wrongly believed my own issues stemming from my childhood made me more effective as a minister to the hurt and fallen. I found power and fearlessness in the anger I could conjure up at a moment's notice and pass it off as God's righteous and just anger. I walked dangerous neighborhoods to spread the Gospel with no fear of my own demise. After all, wouldn't giving my life so that others may be saved, even healed, be what Jesus would do?

But I was not Jesus. Not at all.

I internalized the pain of the poor, homeless, hurting, and downtrodden, carrying their pain on top of mine. I never realized the weight of the burden I carried, nor the reason I was doing it was to not have to deal with my own issues. So, I worked harder, like the ministry all depended on me. Those who coached me loved having a guy who would do whatever it took, at whatever the cost, to save others. Oh, how they enjoyed presenting plaques of honor and leading the church in standing ovations for my sacrifice. They enjoyed how my work reflected so positively on them as my mentors. It finally took its toll and broke my spirit.

I was depressed and exhausted most of the time, sometimes leaving work to battle suicidal thoughts. I couldn't escape the pain of those to whom I ministered and loved. I was an empath run amuck, out of control. I didn't think anyone could understand. Not even Creator.

Unwise.

Finally, I burned out. I left the ministry and my unhealthy care for souls, thinking I was the better for it.

That all changed when Naomi took her life five years after that. I sunk deeper into the mire of a self-blame, further into the depression dungeon I had sentenced myself to forever.

He who blames others has a long way to go on his journey.
He who blames himself is halfway there.
He who blames no one has arrived.

—Chinese Proverb

CHAPTER 10

Confession, Not Always Good for the Soul

We can only tell the truth when we cease to identify with the part of ourselves we think we have to protect.

—*Ram Dass*

I WAS NO angel. I'd only disguised myself as one.

After twenty-three years of a marriage that ended in divorce came the excruciating rawness of being separated from my children. I'll never forget that feeling.

Out of nowhere one Saturday afternoon came a response to my son's angry outburst that left me holding him against the wall by his collar. I don't remember putting him there. Like father like son, I did the very thing I disliked most about my father—mindless rage erupting out of nowhere. A week later, I was asked to leave our home. All I could do at the time was honor the separation in the hope I would return home at some point.

Even so, taking responsibility for wrongs inflicted never lessens the impact of damage done.

A counselor helped me work through the anger, abuse, and violence of my past. It wasn't easy focusing on me when I wanted to feel anger for being exiled from my home and children.

My childhood experiences had trained me well for my self-destructive and self-protecting behaviors. I had never blamed anyone because that had never offered any relief to the pain. But I wanted answers, so I made the only choice that led to peace and began a journey to understand my plight. There was much more going on in the universe than the loss of home and a spotty relationship with my children, neither of which I could do much about at the time anyway.

In the end, I never returned, though it was not my choice.

I sunk into a PTSD form of manic-depression high-lows—sometimes happy and sad in the same moment—in all areas of my life. The flashbacks I experienced only deepened my resolve to get better. Escaping to places of solitude, stillness, and silence with The Great Alone brought the only peace and sanity I could find. In those times, Creator helped me remain relatively optimistic, and I vowed to remain eternally hopeful. It was all I had.

I did not pray for any relief, but I prayed for strength to suffer with courage, humility, and love.

—Brother Lawrence

CHAPTER 11

The Result of Being
an Empath Run Amuck

The greater the perfection a soul aspires after,
the more dependent it is upon Divine Grace.

—*Brother Lawrence*

I FAILED MY first family. I chose to heal the hurts of the world over loving my children and their mother. I was a church planter with a seductive mistress whose name was Miss Ministry. I was guilty of the very thing handed down to me, caring for others more than my own family.

Once, when I was nineteen, I cried out those very words to my father. "You care more about everybody else than you do your own damn family."

His only concern was that I had cursed in his house.

I told him that was the least of the sins committed in his house. The next day, I left for Alaska, carrying in my heart the very thing I hated the most, anger and rage.

I was a lost child.

The effects of the constant bullying, abuse, and violence I had experienced growing up had escalated to the point that I was willing to kill or be killed to protect hurting people, with no concern for my own health and well-being. What did it matter if I was murdered in some dark alley helping a prostitute get off the street or homeless man to a shelter? My mind said no one would care anyway. My heart stayed impassioned for my mission, and my body was tense all the time. My soul was in a constant state of stress and exhaustion. I became, to paraphrase a movie line, a borderline burnout with questionable social skills.

Was my relentless pursuit of justice and serving the downtrodden without restraint or boundaries simply a slow, self-righteous, self-destructive path to suicide?

Thinking back on it, it's not much different than a person who slowly drinks himself to death. Neither was working myself to a frazzle serving the endless needs of hurting people "in the name of God." But that wasn't the worst thing about it.

While I saved the world, I shut out my family.

I couldn't see what I was doing. I just needed to stay ahead of my troubles, like running from a bear that occasionally raked its claws across my back but wasn't quite close enough to take me down. The result was I couldn't manage living in my own home because I couldn't manage myself. I was an unfit husband and father with inner issues no one should have ever had to endure. Trapped, I saw no way out.

The wounds ran deep in this empath junky who soothed his own hurts by caring for others' pain. I once brought to our doorstep an inner-city church member with AIDS who had asked to die in our home.

She said, "I want to die where I know God lives." I'm not sure now how much of God was in that decision.

Early on, doctors were unsure if the virus could be transmitted through the air. While that act of kindness brought praise from every corner of our church denomination, I chanced the safety of my family for a person I'd known only a year. What I didn't realize was that I was teaching Naomi to do the very same thing. But doing good deeds in the most extreme ways were not the only issue with which I wrestled.

My empathy ran deep. Way too deep.

Through the years, I'd experienced recurring empathic visions of soldiers dying in senseless and useless wars. One involved a World War I battle scene while watching TV with the family. Great armies rose from the trenches to go "over the top" into No Man's Land, where machine guns, bombs, and bayonets destroyed the flesh of thousands. In the flash of that split second, I saw the individual face of every man who charged their enemy's position. My soul moaned the loss of all those who could have brought beauty and love into the world. Their deaths were meaningless. My heart wailed for those who could have had good lives with homes and families. In that fleeting vision, every face smiled at first but then turned hollow-eyed and gray, like dead people longing for hope. I saw their anguish. Their pain devastated me. Those mystical moments drained my soul, often leaving me little to no energy for my family.

When the vision that night ended, I burst out, "What's the use?"

My family was startled and sure I had lost my mind. Maybe I had.

Once, while reading Gautama, I experienced an overwhelming sense of how alone Creator must feel, having no one with whom to commune. Upon realizing Creator had been forced to live as The Great Alone since time began, I burst into tears. That I was part of the problem only made my anguish worse.

My visions and tears changed the day after Naomi's death, from experiencing the great loss of human good ruined by wars, violence, abuse, famine, and disease to the grief of how I had neglected and avoided my friendship with Creator. And Naomi. I became an empath run amuck who terribly ruined his family relationships. I not only had abandoned Creator, but my daughter as well.

In the wee hours of one dark night not long after Naomi died, I begged Creator, "Please make a way for me to right this wrong." Immediately, overpowering acceptance and love saturated my body. I cried for myself, for Creator, and for Naomi. But I found my resolve. I wanted Naomi to share in Creator's indescribable love, so I pleaded, "Please, let me help her find Your love on the other side."

Silence.

"Creator, I know I am unfit, but please...."

Creator's Great Voice echoed in my soul, *"Yes, you are. But you must go."*

I understood.

After this, Job opened his mouth and cursed the day of his birth.

—Job 3:1, NIV

The mystic sits inside the burning.

—Rumi

PART FOUR

Seeing What I Could Not See Before

Once upon a time there was a beautiful
sensitive human being.
The world did not see things the way she did.
She felt things deeply.
She felt everyone's sadness.
But little did she know it was her superpower.
The power to raise above the darkness
and help others do the same.
They called her an Empath.

—Jane Lightworker

CHAPTER 12

The Acorn Fell Too Far from This Tree

Love is the core energy that rules everything.

—*John E. Fetzer*

NAOMI LOVED PEOPLE too much. More than I did, I suppose. Neither of us could avoid carrying another's pain, but Naomi never developed a shut-off valve. Neither had I, but I did learn how to decompress by shutting down, reading, or disappearing for hours, even days at a time. Empaths need a way to tune out, but Naomi never learned to do that. Inside, she must have felt like a decomposing body ready to burst open from the putrid effort of trying to medicate her own pain with thoughts and behaviors unnatural to her true self.

My second greatest regret with Naomi was the night I didn't let her sit with me and snuggle. I was just too tired of everyone and everything. All Naomi wanted was the love of her father. I had nothing left to give. I'd given it all to others. That lost opportunity haunts me still.

The greatest regret I'll always remember was when I told teenaged Naomi she had a bad heart. Naomi was being particularly difficult that day. I don't even remember what the problem was at the time, but I was at my wits' end, more with myself than with her. As quickly as the words "bad heart" left my mouth, I tried to grab them back. But it was too late. I had done the damage of a lifetime. The devastation in her eyes was eternal. I'll never get over that mistake. I'm sure Naomi didn't.

If I could only have one more chance to....

A moment of patience in a moment of anger
avoids a thousand moments of sorrow

—Imam Ali

CHAPTER 13

The Downward Spiral

A man has cause for regret only when he sows and no one reaps.

—Charles Goodyear

NAOMI AND I still had a sporadic relationship despite the difficult moments between us. At times, she would come to me with problems that mostly consisted of fender benders, traffic tickets, or money needs. We frequented a favorite city park bench where we sought solutions to her series of dilemmas. I'd help her sift through her options but never got at the underlying causes. I don't think she knew how to voice them.

Busy lives, a divorce from her mother, and Naomi's upcoming marriage that I had little hand in helping with caused us to drift apart. It wasn't until I decided to take a job in another state that she revealed her true heart. She begged me not to leave, so I stayed. But even after making that decision, I rarely heard from her. I tried to make staying work. It didn't. So finally, I left.

Too many memories and too many lost friends over the divorce made it easier to take a ministry job in a city over two hours away. I returned on weekends to visit friends, and Naomi made sure we found a few hours together. Her emotions reminded me of my own highs and lows at her age. After jogging together a couple of miles each Friday I visited, she would lament over her failing marriage, hopeless employment opportunities, and feeling disoriented in a world she never seemed to understand. It wasn't very long before she became less and less available. Our visits tapered off until they ended.

Most of us were taught that God would love us if and when we change. In fact, God loves you so that you can change.

—Richard Rohr

CHAPTER 14

I Failed

Failures are opportunities to fall into something better.

—the author

I T WAS NEVER about Creator's ability to absorb human beings' pain and suffering. It was about me believing that I could, and should, absorb them for Him. Even taking His place at times, doing His job, thinking I could do it. And survive.

Misunderstanding my empathic gift was my own undoing. But that doesn't excuse how I failed Naomi. She was dying inside, and no one around her knew it. I recognized the signs because I'd lived them myself, yet I was somehow blind to her plight. I didn't know enough about my daughter because I didn't know enough about me. The deeper demons within had yet to be revealed and defeated.

When Naomi died, I felt responsible. The pain was so overwhelming, I wanted to die.

When I finally got the details about her death, never could I have imagined Naomi chose me to help her find her true self. That was the word I needed to plan my quest. I knew where I had to go and what it would take to get there. The vision of a tree kept coming to me at times when I least expected it.

My problem going forward to find Naomi was the embarrassing thought that Creator knew about all the weaknesses I had yet to deal with or forgive myself for. I still had many, many snakeskins that needed to be shed and didn't know how to do that.

But my desire to help Naomi find peace was greater than my struggles and feelings of powerlessness. I was willing to learn. I had to find Naomi.

I screamed at the universe, "To hell with my feelings, I'm going." There was no turning back.

———————————

Broken crayons still color the same.

—Trent Shelton

CHAPTER 15

Saving Grace

If we're judged only by the sum of all our failures in life,
then we're all doomed.

—the author

I'M NO SAINT, never claimed to be one, and don't expect to become one in the conventional sense of the word. The saints of old had more chinks in their armor than I ever did. Still, that's not much of a comfort.

During my childhood, darkness had so snuffed out the light within, I had become lost. The clay pot originally shaped and fired by Creator had to be dropped, broken, and fitted back together before a lighted candle could be placed in it. Only then could light be seen through the cracks of a broken but healing life.

In my sorrow, I retreated to deserted and lonely places, sandbars and mountain cabins, often to be with Creator in nature. I centered my soul around the hopeful truth that Creator never gives up on one of His created ones. If I didn't believe that, I probably would have given up on myself a long time ago. Rather, by spending hours and days with The Great Soul of Creator, I found love and forgiveness, acceptance and connectedness.

My saving grace lay in the hope that Creator would put me back together enough that my faint light might at least illuminate Naomi's return path to her true self.

It's all I had to seek and find Naomi.

The wound is the place where the light enters you.

—Rumi

CHAPTER 16

My Undoing

My life never has run in a straight line.

—the author

NEVER WAS THERE a time that I did not love my children. I just didn't know how to show them.

It's pretty easy to tell someone else to simply not be like their parents. It's another thing to not become like them as we grow older. Growing up with an overly doting mother and a father who abused my brothers and me, it's no wonder I wasn't prepared to be a father.

Counselors advised, "Break the chains that hold you. Deal with your past."

That's easier said than done when you're years into your first marriage before you realize that not everyone grew up like you did. Not everyone had parents like John and Olivia on The Waltons. The anger, abuse, and violence I grew up with was generational on both sides. By the time my kids were angry teens, I didn't understand what I had done, or what had been done to me, to cause it.

When my wife at the time asked me to leave home, I wanted to return. Soon, it became clear I never would. I made amends that were neither acknowledged nor accepted. Forgiveness was beyond her capabilities. She feigned wanting to work things out, but after two years, she reversed her desires. I had been duped. She held the past over my head and would not forgive.

The day she finally asked for a divorce, a good friend consoled me, saying, "The greatest sin of all is holding another to a past Creator has already forgiven."

I thought, if God can forgive a wrong, how could she not? She honored no part of that belief.

After I agreed to the divorce, she continued to turn our children against me rather than fostering any chance of reconciliation. I found myself alone with nowhere to turn but the mystical arms of Creator, and in His embrace, I let the chips fall where they may.

Naomi had no such recourse in her downward spiral. Fourteen years after the divorce, Naomi gave up. No one had a clue she was contemplating taking her life. Not her husband, brother, or mother. Or me.

Though completely caught off guard when I received the news she had taken her life, I didn't understand why except that I had struggled with the same decision too many times. It was just that Naomi had acted upon hers.

I can be changed by what happens to me.
But I refuse to be reduced by it.

—Maya Angelou

CHAPTER 17

The Mistake

*Not the ones speaking the same language, but the ones
sharing the same feeling understand each other.*

—*Rumi*

WHEN MOST PEOPLE lose a loved one, the pain they feel is more about the loss they experience than anything else. But for an empath, it's not just personal loss that's mourned. Empaths embody the pain of their lost loved one, even after they pass. Naomi and I shared the same gift and the same unhealthy thoughts and feelings. I just didn't realize the depth of hers.

Sometimes, a gift enjoyed becomes an addiction uncontrolled. That was me, but more so Naomi. Her empathic gift controlled her like an addict frantically fumbling for pills as they slipped through her fingers. She chased what could never satisfy. New hairdo, fancy clothes, the best job. But in so doing, she lost all sense of who she really was. She found no peace to her endless concern for another's well-being. Naomi's pain was so unbearable, she chose to leave it for a better day.

That pain became mine.

Naomi was the greater empath between the two of us. She had the greater need to help others but also a greater need for help herself. That was my mistake, not knowing and not taking the time to find out. I was unaware. That's where I failed.

She couldn't handle the stress of caring for a world not hers.

Just because someone carries it well, doesn't mean it isn't heavy.

—Unknown

A soul that carries empathy is a soul that has survived enormous pain.

—Unknown

CHAPTER 18

The Truth

Truth, though elusive at best, is still best.

—the author

I HAD CHOSEN ministry to mask my inabilities and continued self-willfulness. I believed if I worked hard and long enough, helped the lowest of the low with all my might, and got the recognition I never received from my father, I could stay ahead of the demons hard on my heels trying to destroy me. Demons I foolishly believed I could outrun and defeat.

In my ministry years, I had the noble reputation in our church circles as a champion for the poor and homeless. But inside, I was an over-achieving, self-protecting introvert who gave himself to everyone but his family. Believing my own self-assigned importance, I expected the family to understand and hold me in as high regard as those whom I had fooled in the seen world. It didn't work. The unseen knew better.

I only fooled myself.

I was mistaken.

I lost my family.

I lost my daughter.

She killed herself.

I was lost.

It does not require many words to speak the truth.

—*Chief Joseph*

CHAPTER 19

The Distancing

For things to reveal themselves to us, we need to
be ready to abandon our views about them.

—*Thich Nhat Hanh*

EVEN BEFORE THE divorce from their mother, the seeds of estrangement had already been planted between my children and me. I learned how to live with too many things left unresolved, things I could do nothing about. I had hoped our family could be put back together. It didn't happen.

The day her mother decided she wanted a divorce, Naomi stopped speaking to me. Four months later, she called on Christmas Day, crying and apologizing. The cycle repeated itself several times after that. Pulling me close, then shoving me away. It was nearly more than I could bear.

Four years later, after I had married again, Naomi called crying and apologizing. I didn't discuss the whys of all she brought up. I was just happy to have my daughter back. Naomi visited and called, and she struck up a happy friendship with my step-daughter. But things slowly returned to what I experienced so many times.

She and I had an on-and-off relationship from that point on, depending on the intensity of her relationship with her mother, which wasn't always pleasant. It wasn't how I wanted it to be, but it was better than what I'd had.

Three decades of giving ministry the best of myself finally caught up with me. I burned out. I had no more to give. Naomi was the only one who called to check on me. But that didn't last either. Not long after I resigned from ministry, I texted her a Happy Birthday message.

She responded with a simple, Thanks.

That was my last contact with her before she passed.

Naomi later broke her silence, calling my father one month before she took her life. Dad related how deeply confused and disturbed she seemed, like something had snapped inside her. She had little to say, allowing long silences to stretch between them. When she brought up my name, Dad encouraged her to call and talk to me. She didn't.

It hurt, but I never lost hope that she would reach out.

Naomi gave up less than a month later and ended her life.

To give up yourself without regret is the greatest charity.

—*Bodhidharma*

PART FIVE

Devastation Beyond Measure

Mostly it is loss which teaches us about the worth of things.

—Arthur Schopenhauer

CHAPTER 20

Naomi's Decision

The most terrifying thing is to accept oneself completely.

—Carl Jung

A FEW YEARS after the divorce, Naomi asked me, with no harm intended, "Dad, you just don't do family very well, do you?" By then, I think she understood my unhealthy upbringing had pretty much negated any chance of my doing family very well. I think she was trying to say she felt the same way about her own family experience.

Naomi said, "I'm not very good at it either, Dad."

All I could say was, "I never knew how, nor took the time to learn. I'm truly sorry about that."

She cocked her head and said, "I guess we're more alike than I knew."

Our empathic souls connected in that moment. She understood without judging. She asked about things that happened to me when I was growing up. I didn't realize the damage our conversation was having on her.

She absorbed the pain of too many people. She absorbed mine that day. It was more than she could bear.

After years of carrying others' burdens, Naomi came to a decision I had pondered several times myself—to end her life.

I didn't act on it.

She did.

Life was too much for Naomi, so she checked out for a better day.

And I, too, did what I always did. I checked out.

Your body is away from me, but there is a window open from my heart to yours.

—Rumi

CHAPTER 21

The Call

Hardships often prepare ordinary people for an extraordinary destiny.

—*C.S. Lewis*

A N UNEXPECTED PHONE call with a strange area code popped up on my phone at eight o'clock that Friday night, March 15. When I answered, the kids' mother simply said, "Our daughter has shot herself." Naomi's mother sniffled, asked if I had someone with me, and said she would call after she arrived at the scene of Naomi's death and had more information. She was uncharacteristically kind.

After that brief conversation, I hung up the phone, devastated. I almost passed out. In those few seconds, my emotions rocketed from deep woundedness to extreme hurt to uncontrollable rage. I stood up and screamed words I don't remember. I told my wife the news as I marched to the most convenient piece of furniture, her grandmother's antique rocking chair. I raised it over my head with every intention of smashing it to bits. But I caught myself and carefully set the chair back down. I returned to my recliner, then crumpled low into the seat.

My wife and I agonized for over two hours for a call from Naomi's mother that never came. We could wait no longer. We packed a few things, including a suit for me in case a funeral was in our future. We stopped two hours later to get wiper fluid to wash away the myriad of bugs plastered on the windshield. I wanted something to wash away the pain plastered on my heart. There was nothing for that anywhere.

As we exited the store, Naomi's mother called. "She's gone," in her characteristic distanced voice that revealed she would no longer be kind.

All I could choke out was, "I am so sorry."

She blurted out curtly, "Well, so am I!"

I knew what that meant.

She blamed me for Naomi's death. I couldn't think and didn't know what to say.

"What should I do?" I wanted to be with my daughter even though I didn't feel that would be the best thing to say. I didn't know what to say.

"What do you mean, what should you do?" Grace and kindness were exchanged for blame and hate.

"Well, we're on our way to where you are. I want to be there with—"

"Naomi's husband doesn't want to see you."

How could that be when I'd never even met the guy? Really, I knew.

Then, she spoke in the monotone voice of an executioner. "And I'm sure our son doesn't want to see you, either. But I'll call and see."

She hadn't hung up thirty seconds when the phone rang again. I answered, "Hello?"

A pause ensued. I felt the demons circling.

"*You* can turn around and go home." I'd never heard her voice sound so pleased. And I know she never called our son.

Shocked, disoriented, hurt, and confused, all I could mumble was some unintelligible gibberish. Realizing any more conversation was fruitless, I simply gave a stern, "Goodbye."

Darkness thickened. Hysterical sounds of demons laughing clogged my mind. I couldn't see straight. I needed light.

I began formulating a plan to find it.

Sometimes, you'll have to make peace with the idea
of being seen as the villain of the story,
in order to stand for your highest truth.

—Xavier Dagba

PART SIX

Preparation

---

*No matter how long you have traveled in the wrong direction,
you can always turn around.*

—Unknown

---

*The bend in the road is not the end of the road...
Unless you fail to make the turn.*

—Helen Keller

---

*Courage is not having the strength to go on,
it's going on when you don't have the strength.*

—Teddy Roosevelt

———————

What we plant in the soil of contemplation we shall reap in the harvest of action.

—Meister Eckhart

———————

Stop acting so small. You are the universe in ecstatic motion.

—Rumi

CHAPTER 22

Regrets—the Stuff of Death and Life

In all this, Job did not sin by charging God with wrongdoing.

—Job 1:22, NIV

L IFE IN THIS world is fleeting at best, and I wasted much of the time I had with Naomi. Regrets are memories slipping through wishful fingers grasping at should haves and could haves. Regrets serve only to depress the already beleaguered mind. Naomi's death shook the fruit of regrets from the tree of poor fathering, and I was all too happy to gather them into my basket, unhealthy, self-assigned blame at its best. In my mind, I knew I was not responsible for Naomi's choice to end her life, but my heart said otherwise.

Once the immediate shock of Naomi's death subsided, I wracked my brain for all I had done wrong as a father. It wasn't the involuntary thoughts that sickened me. No, I sought the worst of what I'd done that could have contributed to her decision. And I didn't have far to look.

I was no hero in this story. In many ways, I was the villain. The demons that had blocked my knowing who Naomi was then would be the same that would keep me from finding her on the other side now if I didn't deal with them.

I had to face myself.

It wasn't easy.

I wasn't some great hero for doing it.

If anyone was the hero, it was Naomi. I wanted to find her, apologize for my failure, and help her find her place in the Universe. I didn't come up with the idea. That belonged to One who knows me best and loves me most. The One I've trusted without question—Creator.

To regret deeply is to live afresh.

—Wesley Gosslein

CHAPTER 23

Resigned to the Fact

The final stage of healing is using what happens to you
to help other people.

—Gloria Stein

IN THE DAYS after Naomi's passing, I wasn't just sad for my loss. I also absorbed her painful death as well as my estranged son's and ex-wife's sorrow. More than that, I breathed in the anguish for all Naomi lost by leaving this world at such a young age. And for what the world will never get to experience because of the void she left behind.

I was the empath run amuck. Again.

Yet I found hope knowing she was still alive somewhere in the universe.

One night, I awoke to hear a voice. I couldn't understand the words but knew what to ask. "Where are you, Naomi?"

Only the wind outside my window answered. *Here, there, everywhere.*

For months, I prayed for what to do. I settled on one answer. I must go and find Naomi.

I wanted her to find life, even if I lost mine in the process.

I wanted to teach her to navigate the obstacles put in her way long before she was born.

Naomi came into the world with no experience of combatting demons that should've never been hers in the first place. I wanted to stand between them and her so she could escape their grasp. They had to be defeated if she was to live in a world Creator had prepared her for.

I decided I would go.

I would help set her free.

I would take her place forever if necessary. I was willing.

Faith is standing in the place of unknowing and refusing to leave.

—the author

CHAPTER 24

The Change

Creator said, "I must drop you."
The Clay Pot cried, "But I will break into a thousand pieces!"
"Yes, you will."
"But why?" the Clay Pot asked.
Creator consoled, "That my light may show through the cracks after I
put you back together."

—the author

I'VE NEVER BEEN an angel, but I'd have to become one to finish this quest. There's a very fine line between good and evil, between being an angel or a demon. I've served with both. More in the camp of the latter, I think. But I was convinced I could change and be a force for good.

I understood an angel of the Creator to be a spiritual being created in light, so that truth would be the foundation of their relationship. To find Naomi, I'd have to face the truth about the part of me that still skulked in the shadows. I had to boldly and honestly enter the light. That wouldn't be easy, and I would need help. What I had to face possessed fangs and slithered in the darkness.

Only true light could part the shadows to make a path through the darkness that gripped me. I had a long way to go to become a bearer of light.

I couldn't do it myself.

I trusted that Creator could change me.

I had to be broken. Only Creator could put me back together.

Only then could Creator's light shine through the cracks of my weakness once he put me back together.

I knew what I had to do. I had to keep repeating that phrase. I was in the cave with King David when he was running from King Saul where the Scriptures say, "But David encouraged himself in the Lord his God."

Take the first step through the thin veil into the unknown. It was time to go.

When a train goes through a tunnel and it gets dark,
you don't throw away the ticket and jump off.
You sit still and trust the engineer.

—Corrie Ten Boom

CHAPTER 25

Three Dreams

Death ends a life, not a relationship.

—*Jack Lemmon*

DREAMS ARE WINDOWS into the way the mind tries to make sense of the world. Though scattered and elusive, their meanings always possess a kernel of wisdom. Three dreams prepared me for my quest to find Naomi.

The first came in the fall after Naomi's death.

A week before the first birthday after her passing, I woke to shivering chills racing from head to toe. I only experienced that when evil was present. The dream escaped me but not its effects. Suddenly, all the wrongs I'd ever done paraded themselves before me. Faint laughter reminded of a familiar voice I'd heard many times. Suicidal thoughts sent my mind scurrying to take action. Since Naomi's death, they had become more frequent. The demons' voices were much more inviting that morning.

I chanted an ancient prayer forged by mystics in the fires of spiritual battle. "Lord Jesus Christ, have mercy on me, a sinner." I rarely repeated the last two words because I didn't claim sinner as my identity. That morning, I did. I needed grace.

Hanging myself, swallowing a bottle of sleeping pills, or drowning in the Mississippi River were the usual choices in these moments. But a new method presented itself early that morning. The loaded pistol in my bedroom crossed my mind. I stared at it sitting on the closet shelf but refused to take hold of it. I never intended to. I faced my sorrow and defeated the notion of turning the gun upon myself. I had something to live for. Or rather, die for.

I tried to write. It didn't help. I fixed a cup of whiskey on ice to ease the pain. I'd never done that before, but it worked. I slept most of the day. By evening, I felt much better, or so I thought. Becoming an alcoholic wouldn't be all that difficult. The next morning, the pain was back. I poured the whiskey down the drain and threw the bottle in the trash.

The second dream came a week before Thanksgiving.

Naomi and my son were seated at the breakfast table in the last house where we all lived together. My son laughed and talked as usual, but Naomi was white from head to toe, like she had been bleached. Even her eyes were solid white. When I called her name, she grinned slightly. When I hugged her, she was cold and lifeless. Then, it hit me. She was visiting from the grave.

I immediately was spirited away to my parents' living room when I was a teenager. Dad sat in his favorite chair, my older brother in my mother's chair, and my younger brother on the love seat. I sat in the chair next to the TV, with the best view of the other three. My mother sat in a hard, straight-back chair behind my father, covering her face with her hands.

Dad joked about how badly he treated us when we were kids.

My older brother, who'd received the worst of Dad's abuse, snickered contemptuously. "Yeah, old man, laugh it up."

Dad stopped with a start and teared up. "If only that thing back in 1951 hadn't happened, I never would've been like this."

I wanted to know what thing it was, but I awoke before I could ask him. There it was, finally a clue to why Dad treated us so poorly.

Something had severely affected him in 1951. Whatever it was, it tied all of this mess together. I didn't need to know what happened. I just needed to know that something did happen.

The last of the three dreams occurred on New Year's morning before the first anniversary of Naomi's death.

I was feeling depressed already. In the dream, I had traveled back in time knowing that Naomi had taken her life. I found her in the home where we lived when she was only three years old. I hugged and kissed her, but when I held her tight, she disappeared. I woke up empty-armed and broken-hearted. I cried into my pillow until it was soaked.

I couldn't make any sense of my upside-down world in that moment, so I asked myself, How does this New Year's Day feel with Naomi gone?

I answered aloud. "Terrible, insurmountable grief and pain. Getting beyond the past is like dragging a huge ship anchor across the ocean floor, while drowning at the same time."

Then, I asked myself, *Just how deep runs the woundedness of my past?*

Again, I spoke my reply. "Like being violently sucked down into the bottomless funnel of a dark, violent tornado. I keep spinning but can't break free."

The only way I would break free from the past was to help set Naomi free for her future.

I had to change.

On the run.

And become a better person.

Like in a fairytale, but with the possibility of no happily ever after.

It's no use going back to yesterday because
I was a different person then.

—Alice in Wonderland

PART SEVEN

Taking the First Step

When you do things from your soul, you feel a river moving in you, a joy.

—*Rumi*

Life has taught me that the people who have been broken the most,are usually the ones who go out of their way to put others back together.

—*Bianca Sparacino*

CHAPTER 26

Searching for the Name Tree

Not all who wander are lost.

—J. R. R. Tolkien

Since Naomi's death, I've wanted to sit beside the Name Tree where her name was carved. Finding it would give me strength to take the big step into the world where she now lived.

The first time I tried, I was unsure if I should even be there. With the pandemic restrictions lifted, I had more confidence in this second trip to find the Name Tree. I set out early on a Sunday morning. It felt right this time.

On the way, a spiritual friend messaged me. *Ask to be guided in the right direction.*

As I steered my truck onto the state park road, my chest tightened, and my guts rolled. Fifteen minutes later, I strapped on my hiking boots and loaded my small backpack with a bottle of water and a laminated picture of Naomi sitting in front of the Name Tree I took the day I carved the letters into the towering old beech. I grabbed my walking stick, then started my descent. It'd been many years since Naomi and I found the Name Tree. Naomi and I didn't get back to the Name Tree as we'd planned. Like I had hoped. That was a mistake.

I eased down a gentle slope that didn't look too familiar.

Peace descended upon me as I worked my way down the two-hundred-foot bluffs into the hollow. I passed a number of beech trees with names carved in them, some dating back decades. I poured over each one hoping to find Naomi's name. But I knew better. I had to go farther. Once at the bottom, I decided to work my way to the cottonwood flats and explore each gully in the cliff line until I found the Name Tree.

I had no doubt I'd find the tree. I just kept looking.

As I searched the second hollow, a torrential rain exploded like someone had dumped a gigantic bucket of water from the sky. I waited under a cottonwood tree until the downpour let up. My drenched clothes hung heavy. My soul heavier.

Once the storm passed, I wandered out from the bluff line into the flats to stand in the sun as the trees dripped. I wanted to go one direction but felt pulled to go the other way. When I turned, a spirit of light passed by me in a flash, but not so quickly that I couldn't make out the shape. Like a wisp of smoke, she swept past, wearing long flowing robes that gently fluttered in the air. A gentle voice cooed past me like a mourning dove calling for rain in a drought.

I wasn't frightened, but I was startled. "Oh, my goodness. What was that?" The encounter caught me off guard when I should've expected to have visitors.

Her form was clear and face familiar. There was no wind, but I felt the unhurried warm gust when she passed by. Leaves on the sapling next to me danced as though a gentle breeze swayed its branches. She traveled in the direction of the course I'd chosen. Verification? I collected myself. I'd learned not to make too much about the things I had been allowed to see. I took them as they came, and if I was to know more, Creator would reveal it. But I had a good idea of who she was—Granny.

Suddenly, the sun burst through the dark clouds, brightening the forest. I kept going, exploring each hollow and checking every trunk that could possibly have been the Name Tree.

Not long after the spirit visited, I found what I believed to be the Name Tree. "Could this really be it?"

Though it had been struck by lightning, the Name Tree looked healthy. "Granny, is this a sign?"

A voice through the shadowy wood echoed, *"The one suffering voluntary purification becomes the healthiest of souls. Death precedes resurrection. Truth must be uncovered to be rewritten."*

That gave me hope.

I checked the tree over for Naomi's name. A charred ribbon made by the lightning had wrapped around the tree like the stripes on a peppermint stick. The bark where the letters of Naomi's name should've been was charred.

I took out the old photo I'd brought with me of when Naomi and I found the Name Tree so many years ago. I compared backgrounds. I was in the right place. I had found the Name Tree. I did a double-take of the picture. Behind Naomi, a face with my features moved, like in a video—hair long like I wore it years ago, dark complexion, gold wire rimmed glasses, and a dark mustache. I glanced at the tree and back at the picture. The face was still there but had stopped moving. Then, it hit me. It was my face at the time I took the picture.

I sat by the tree for a while, rubbing the burned bark where the letters of Naomi's name would have been carved. "This is the Name Tree. I'm sure of it."

The words had barely left my mouth when a violent storm rolled in with lightning brightening the forest like a Friday night football game. Blasts of thunder grumbled like an angry old man. All became still. Rain pounded like a herd of horses thundering my way, pouring down harder than the previous time. I stayed by the Name Tree. If lightning struck the Name Tree again and me with it, so be it.

I wasn't leaving.

No force in the seen world or marshaled against me from the unseen would drive me away. I wanted whatever truth there was to be had, whatever gem of wisdom that could be mine, to help me on my way to find Naomi. I knew this storm would prepare me for the next one. The one that would take me through the thin veil.

Satisfied that I had found the Name Tree in this life, I was fully confident I would find it—and Naomi—in the next.

Finally, the storm gave up. But I had not.

The Name Tree wasn't easy to find.

But I found it.

With help.

I knew then I would not travel through the thin veil alone.

I would find the Name Tree on the other side.

And Naomi.

I CRAWLED UP out of the steep gully walls in the light rain, slipping, sliding, and twisting my bad knee. At the top, I soaked in the sunshine sneaking through the vanishing clouds, the first part of my quest satisfied. I had found the Name Tree.

I prayed, "Creator, I don't know what all I just experienced, but thank you."

You are not meant to avoid the darkness. You are meant to go into it, feed it love, illuminate it and transform it into light. Only love has the power to heal the darkness within you.

—Alyonna Parveen

CHAPTER 27

Affirmation Springs from the Best of Creation

Nothing ever goes away until it teaches us what we need to know.

—*Pema Chodron*

O N THE DRIVE home, I realized my quest in that forest was never about finding the tree with Naomi's name carved in it. Rather, it was about navigating the forest and finding the tree through the thin veil where she could be set free. I had to go to the Name Tree in the unseen realm.

At dawn the next morning, a red cardinal appeared on a limb just outside the window where I write. It began the prettiest serenade I'd heard in a long time. I could almost hear Naomi's voice in the song and sense her presence in the fluttering of his wings. It was the first of many visits.

Since ancient times, across a number of cultures, people have held sacred traditions associated with red birds. Their messages from the spirit world always involve something noteworthy, like warnings about illness or harm, or pointing a traveler in the right direction. Tradition has it that a person can speak a message to the east, and a red cardinal will carry the message.

As the red cardinal sang, I spoke a message to the east. I asked Naomi for forgiveness, then told her I loved her and would see her soon.

My last words were, "Naomi, I'm coming."

The cardinal immediately ended his song and flew away into the deep woods. To the east.

Message sent.

Because it is not what you are nor what you have been
that God looks at with his merciful eyes, but what you desire to be.

—The Cloud of Unknowing

CHAPTER 28

My Decision

Whatever the present moment contains, accept it as if you had chosen it. Always work with it, not against it.

—*Eckhart Tolle*

HOW COULD I prepare to enter the next world? There were no travel guides for such a venture.

Suicide. That's what people will say. Because they want the quickest and simplest explanation so they can get on about their lives. Move on and forget. I long ago gave up swallowing so-called interpreters of God's Word when the Universe told me something else.

Despite what biblical scholars and good church folks teach, Hell isn't the only destiny possible for those who take their lives. If a person can be forgiven for killing himself through alcohol, drugs, or in a car crash because of a need for speed or rage, then suicide can be forgiven as well. If not, obese buffet stuffers and addicts of every stripe won't have a snowball's chance in hell of getting to heaven. The only difference is they killed themselves slowly.

Finding Naomi required a sacrifice beyond what most would deem right and reasonable. Having thrown reasonable to the wind long ago, I decided to dive into the tumultuous sea of wild spiritual currents and dangerous monsters to help my daughter who had fallen overboard. Reasonable wasn't even part of the discussion. Helping Naomi find true life could be done no other way. I trusted Creator understood my intentions.

So, I decided to do just that.

I never saw myself as committing suicide. Rather, I readied myself to become an astronaut launching into unknown space with little chance of returning home. The discovery would be worth the sacrifice.

It was clear that I had to travel through the thin veil—now.

I wasn't leaving because I was hopeless or for some noble cause poets love to write about. I loved my child and was willing to do whatever it took to help her. I had prayed, meditated, sought the wisdom of the ancients, did a tarot card reading with a beloved friend, and even considered seeking out a medium through whom I might reach out to Naomi.

A medium? Honestly? Not really.

I had sat long enough with Job, scraping my sores with a potsherd. I offered myself to my Creator as a servant to open the door to a life Naomi was always supposed to live.

It was a very easy decision once my mind was made up.

There's courage involved if you want to become truth.

—Rumi

PART EIGHT

Through the Thin Veil I Traveled

It's impossible, said pride.
It's risky, said experience.
It's pointless, said reason.
Give it a try, whispered the heart.

—Unknown

All shall be well, and all shall be well, and all manner of thing
shall be well... for there is a force of love moving through
the universe that holds us fast and will never let us go.

—St. Julian of Norwich

CHAPTER 29

Day of Days

Death is the protector of life and life is the process of death.

—Wasif Ali Wasif

MARCH 15. ONE year to the day after Naomi took her life. That is when, resolved and determined, I began my quest to find Naomi.

She wouldn't know I was coming. I wasn't sure if she'd want to see me when I arrived. It was a chance I was willing to take.

I had been chosen.

I wanted to apologize.

I wanted to hold my daughter one more time like I didn't do that regretted night.

I would have to see beyond my failures as a father.

I wanted Naomi found and set free.

I would have to change.

I trusted Creator would give me a second chance to be what I always wanted to be.

What He intended all along.

Naomi's father.

———————

MY MIND FOUND peace.

My heart experienced tranquility.

My soul melded with The Great Soul.

My body was ready.

Just one last thing left to do.

Humility in itself is nothing else but true knowledge and experience of yourself as you are.

—The Cloud of Unknowing

CHAPTER 30

The Farewell Letter

Never say goodbye, because saying goodbye means going away,
and going away means forgetting.

—Peter Pan

I wrote the farewell letter to my wife that Naomi did not write to me. I didn't know what to say, so I just started writing.

Babe, how do I tell you I'm leaving but love you more than life itself? I know that like most things I've talked about lately, this doesn't make any sense. I haven't been myself since Naomi died. I know you understand, but still, for the long periods of sadness and distancing myself, I'm sorry. You're the most understanding person I've ever met. Thanks for sticking by me in the toughest of times. Not many wives would have.

What you may not understand now is I have to go. I'm not leaving because life is too hard or that my depression has completely overwhelmed me. In fact, it's quite the opposite. You are the best thing Creator has ever gifted me with in this life. And now, I have to give you back.

You know Naomi has been calling my name, and I have to go find her. She's more lost now than before she took her life. I'm not leaving because the pain of her passing is too great. I'm going to find Naomi. I'm going to help her. And in the process, maybe I'll be saved, too.

You know where I'll be—at the Name Tree. You should be able to follow the map.

I love you with all my heart, but this I have to do. One prayer from you will see me through.

Please tell our other daughter I'm sorry I won't be there for the birth of her first child.

I'll be waiting for you when you pass through the thin veil.

I signed the note and left a map on the kitchen table where she could find them.

A short prayer pierces heaven.

—The Cloud of Unknowing

CHAPTER 31

My Last Earthly Descent

The price of inaction is far greater than the cost of making a mistake.

—Meister Eckhart

I REFLECTED ON many things during the drive. I parked in the very same spot above the deep hollow Naomi and I did so many years ago when we found the Name Tree. With my small backpack shouldered, I worked my way down the same trail we had taken together so many years ago to the Name Tree. Unsure and nervous, I followed the same trickling brook that led to the great old beech tree with the burnt lightning stripes. I hadn't noticed my surroundings much when I came last. Granny's visitation, finding the Name Tree, and the darkness of the storms on my last visit had captivated my attention. The canopy above now blocked the sun because the trees had filled out considerably. But the terrain was still deep and rugged, even foreboding.

A warm presence surrounded me.

I stopped. "There you are." I admired the great old tree and traced every high branch and limb all the way down to the trunk, where I decided to sit as my final resting place.

With no warning, overwhelming doubt pressed down on me.

"I can't do this." I stood still as a deer staring into the headlights, wondering if I could go forward. Questioning whether I should. Paralyzed.

But I'd come with a purpose. I sucked in a deep breath and took a few more steps.

An unexpected anger raised its head like a dragon from its hellish dungeon. "Why do I have to do this?"

No parting of the clouds. No angels singing a hallelujah chorus. No answer burst forth from the sky. Nothing.

I stumbled my way through the final short stretch, losing strength with every step. Each became heavier. When I stopped in front of the ancient beech tree and touched its smooth, gray bark, heavy clouds overshadowed the hollow like a bad storm approached. The weight of a thousand millstones pressed down hard against my shoulders. Debilitating inadequacy within struck me down.

"I'm not strong enough." My legs collapsed, and I landed hard on all fours. "This is impossible."

The puddle of dancing crystal clear water of the tiny stream reflected the face of an old, decomposing man with white hair, who would've looked better in a morgue. I snapped back as though a snake had struck at me. I couldn't look. But I had to. There would be no other way. I had no other plan. Then, I took a good look into the pure sparkling pool at me.

"That's what I looked like inside. Dead."

I crawled to the trunk of the tree and settled between two large exposed roots, gray and smooth. After collecting myself, I kneeled and stared at the trunk, wishing Naomi's name was there. The patch of burnt bark where the letters would have been was gone. Large, distorted letters had stretched twice their original size over the years in the flesh of the tree.

Where did those come from?

Naomi's name was barely legible but readable. Why I didn't see them on my last visit? Maybe I wasn't ready to see them. The burned bark had been cleared away to reveal each letter scratched deep into the wood.

A voice whispered into my soul, *"You are ready."*

I traced her name with my finger. N-A-O-M-I. Each letter spoke a sweet memory of Naomi's life. I gently pressed my cheek and ear against the rough wood and scorched bark. I listened. Everything around stood motionless—the leaves, the trickling of the small stream, and my unsettled soul.

A small voice assured me, "You can."

I whispered back, "I will."

I sat and relaxed with my back against the tree underneath Naomi's carved name.

A slight rustling made me look at what I thought, moments ago, was a rock not six feet away. A large copperhead uncoiled, then slithered away into the forest.

"Still showing up to disturb Creator's work, aren't you, old Accuser? Not today, Satan. But I will pray for you."

Once you make a decision, the universe conspires to make it happen.

—Ralph Waldo Emerson

CHAPTER 32

The Exit

We only have to go a little beyond the frontier of sensible appearances in order to see the divine.

—*Pierre Teilhard Chardin*

DARK CLOUDS WEAKENED my resolve, but the tune of the trickling stream strengthened the courage to begin my search. "If that stream trusts Creator to go where it does not know, so can I." The bubbling calmed my soul.

"Creator, will you go with me?"

Silence.

"I know. It's that free-will thing. Well then, here goes nothing. And everything." I chased a handful of prescription pain pills with a slug of fine Scotch whiskey.

A familiar voice whispered, *"I'm already there."*

"How long will I—"

"After the third day, you shall rise if you truly seek the death of your own making."

My eyes blinked. I slumped against the tree more comfortably. I couldn't help it. I had to send my wife a text to tell her one last time that I loved her.

Didn't matter. She wouldn't know to come find me until long after I had embarked on my quest. After I hit send, the phone slid from my hand.

Visions of Naomi dancing and singing in a field of wildflowers rolled through my mind. I could tell I was smiling. But the rest of my body? Nothing. I sensed the forest surrounding me where I sat, but also a place somewhere else. One faded into the other. I was in the *in between*, passing through the thin veil.

I recited my favorite verse, "Be still and know that I am God." I hummed "Amazing Grace" until I heard the sounds of the forest no more. I counted on both when my eyes finally closed.

My soul asked, "Are you there?"

"*I am*," a gentle whisper offered.

––––––––––––––

New beginnings are often disguised as painful endings.

—Lao Tzu

PART NINE
Blessed Jesus, Hold My Hand

No one really knows why they are alive
until they know what they'd die for.

—Martin Luther King, Jr.

Circle me, Lord. Keep protection near and danger afar.
Circle me, Lord. Keep hope within. Keep doubt without.
Circle me, Lord. Keep light near and darkness afar.
Circle me, Lord. Keep peace within. Keep evil out.

—Rev. David Adam

And I said, "Here am I. Send me!"
—Isaiah 6

CHAPTER 33

The Arrival

As the river enters the ocean, so my heart touches Thee.

—Kabir

M
Y HEAD BOBBED only once, like a fishing cork on a still pond. My eyes immediately opened as though being startled from a long, deep, restful sleep.

Ripples of my presence tsunamied across the landscape upon my arrival, like a huge rock dropped into a lake of unknown depth. I had passed through the thin veil. It was as if the entire Universe awoke to my landing. My every human sense burned alive as if I was experiencing it for the first time. Every pore in my skin perceiving, every smell drawn in sweet and foul, every splash of color sharp and blinding, every sound distinguishable, the very air palatable to the tongue. Every part of me pulled in all that surrounded me, and the Universe pulled everything out of me. I tasted the breeze with my tongue, at once both sweet and bitter. Here, I blended with all things surrounding me. Made no effort, just knew. I was aware of everything. I was one with the Universe like never before, more alive in this place than I'd ever been in the land of the living. But wasn't I dead?

Nothing looked familiar, but I knew exactly where I was—beyond death, on the other side of the thin veil. I tried to focus. One tiny spot was clear, directly in front of me. The edges were blurry, like I was looking through an old timey, hand-held telescope. The scene changed constantly, like a kid's kaleidoscope. My eyes blinked like fluttering butterflies. My vision came into focus.

"Uh-oh, this isn't good. No pearly gate or street of gold. No crystal sea and no great throne." Why wasn't I nervous? I really hadn't expected to see those things upon my arrival. I was just relieved not to have landed in a burning lake of fire surrounded by the gnashing teeth of the damned. Funny how I still clung to those old pieces of poor theology. Anyway, I had arrived, and there was no going back. I quieted my anxiety, then stepped forward, floating more than walking.

A great sound boomed forth. *"Forty days and forty nights your tribulation shall be."*

Was that literal or metaphoric? My seminary training wasn't helping.

The whispering wind called, *"Are the simplest of truths still troublesome for you?"*

"It's just… that's a long time." I sighed.

A second boom blasted. *"What is time, but that I am its Master?"* A gale-like surge of energy lifted me up, then set me down. *"Renewed,"* came the call from the sky.

My body was like a twenty-one-year-old's again. I wanted to skip across fields like a kid getting out of school for the summer. I studied my hands and bare feet. "I'll take whatever Creator offers. I need all the help I can get." So, I skipped along on a smooth, dirt path, bouncing like a young rabbit without a care in the world.

A swinging bridge appeared before me, spanning a great canyon with no bottom. The bridge went forth but had no other side.

I stopped in mid-skip. "Something isn't right about this place."

Five hideous demons wearing snakeskin coats, each with a huge letter painted in red on their chests, crawled up on top of five large stone pillars to block my path. Cold shivers marched up and down my back like a thousand cold snakes slithering around my spine.

Each demon screamed its one letter in unison with the others, but I only heard the word, "φ-O-B-O-$\sum$! φ-O-B-O-$\sum$!" They swayed back and forth like caged predators just set free, readying themselves for the kill.

"I know that word. What is that?" I popped the side of my head with my palm and racked my brain. At last, I remembered.

"φOBO$\sum$. Yes, that's it. Fear."

The demons pointed at me, laughed at me uncontrollably, and then chanted, "You said the word. You said the word. You are defeated before you start."

The five pillars combined to become four, as did the demons. They grew longer arms and legs with razor sharp claws, appearing even fiercer. The letters on their chests now spelled F-E-A-R in my handwriting.

A Great Voice shook the ground beneath my feet and rumbled, *"Admit the word, and you may enter."*

"Admit what?"

"That which you have denied for too long."

Rubbing my chin, I whispered, "What should I do? Fight the fear? No. Deny it? No. That I'd denied it for too long. Besides, the Great Voice does sound familiar. I trust that voice. If it takes confessing a fear I did not feel, then so be it. Dad had pretty much beaten the fear out of my brothers and me growing up. Fear is fear though, whether I feel it or not. It's not about feeling as much as it is acknowledging it."

The Great Voice approved. *"You're beginning to understand."*

"I just want to get to Naomi. I'll do anything." I considered everything that came to mind, the cost, the risk, but all led to one conclusion. I was going to have to allow myself to be vulnerable in a place where I wanted to exert the false power of anger I had relied on for so long.

The Great Voice declared, *"That which you have relied on has been the lie. What have you denied under the cover of a false power, which is no power at all?"*

I spoke with power. I was not bashful about my confession. "What, that I'm afraid?"

"*Confession opens any door to truth. You may pass.*"

"That was a lot easier than I would've imagined." I took the gift and pressed on.

Darkness fell heavier than a cold, wet, heavy blanket tossed over my head. I could barely make out the path stretching to the pillars. Many footprints of varying sizes had left their mark on this path, but at different points, they all turned back.

"Whose tracks are these, may I ask?"

A tiny voice so familiar spoke from a swirling cloud of rainbow colors, like a living agate stone. "*You started many times but never chose to finish.*"

"When? I don't remember that."

"*It's never been about the when of the past you now hide yourself behind. It's only the now of the past that you must face.*"

"But the past is what got me here." I wanted to give up. Should I just turn back? But how could I not continue? Naomi was ahead. Out there. Somewhere. I could feel her presence.

The small voice became louder, and the cloud boiled with thunder. "*Will you make the journey?*"

I didn't answer.

The four demons descended the pillars. They surrounded me like a pack of hyenas ready for the final blow to kill and devour their prey.

The ugliest one cackled, "You've got that right."

They read the fear plaguing my unsettled mind. I closed my eyes so I couldn't see the demons as I blindly felt my way through the pillars.

The tiny voice whispered, "*That's what faith is.*"

Clammy clawed hands caressed my arms, legs, and face as they moved up and down my body like a masseuse applying oil before a massage. Lips smacking and teeth grinding made me feel like a prized hog being studied as to how best to be slaughtered, cooked, and consumed.

As they whispered evil wishes and predicted failed outcomes for my journey ahead, I straightened and planted my feet.

One demon fell to its knees, mocking a prayer. "Oh, great Creator, you know this wicked man never loved his daughter or his family. He loved himself more than them, especially more than her."

The four joined together to sing in unison, "He loved himself more than her. He loved himself more than her. And you will never find her. You will never find her." Each demon's face became mine at different times in my life, when I had made poor and selfish choices that hurt Naomi.

Anger stiffened my resolve as I turned away to try and empty myself of unwanted thoughts.

The demons heckled more. "We like anger. Anger is useful. But you know that already."

The angrier I got, the slower my steps became. I flexed my muscles, thinking, *I've got this.*

The demons cried out, "You're not as strong as you think you are."

I quieted myself and pushed the anger down deep.

The demon leader cackled like a witch. "Good, we'll certainly see that again."

———————————

Remember... the entrance to the sanctuary is inside you.

—Rumi

CHAPTER 34

An Unexpected Though Familiar Guide

She who walked the path before you did is the best of guides.

—*the author*

THE WORDS HAD barely left the demon's fanged mouth when I screamed at the top of my lungs. "I did it!"

I confessed everything I could remember anger had done to destroy my life. It took a while. I fell to my knees. My life's energy drained like I was having a major hypoglycemic moment. I couldn't keep my eyes open. I fell to all fours, shaking my head, trying to right myself. I caught my reflection in a muddy puddle on the ground. My skin was pale, and my lips were turning green.

Am I dying? What am I saying? I am dead.

My body listed like a ship about to sink when a weathered, wrinkled old hand gently placed a smooth rock in my mouth. A familiar voice whispered, "Take this. It will sustain you."

I didn't have the strength to even lift my head. "I can't do this. I'm not strong enough."

"No. You are not if you think you can depend upon anger for your strength and power."

With each draw on the stone, new strength and energy traveled from the top of my head to the ends of my fingers and tips of my toes. My vision cleared, and my thinking sharpened. I stood renewed, strong, and at peace, determined to go forward. My soul generated a power not of my own.

But where was the one with the wrinkled old hand who gave me the stone? I knew that voice. I wanted to talk with her. I needed help. The faint edges of a flowing gown, like the one I'd seen in the forest where I found the Name Tree, trailed into the darkness.

Just before she disappeared, I recognized the face that turned and smiled as her gown glowed with the radiance of a living and moving polished agate.

"Granny?" I took the stone from my mouth. It glowed like her gown with the wavy marks of a multicolored agate, continuously shifting. "Will I see you again?"

Granny disappeared before the words left my mouth.

In each of us a different part of the mystery becomes luminous. To truly become yourself, you need the ancient radiance of others.

—John Donohue

CHAPTER 35

Stepping Over My Own Grave

The only thing worse than being blind is having sight with no vision.

—Helen Keller

STRENGTHENED, I FOCUSED on going forward like a mule with blinders, brushing aside the clammy clawed hands and feet of the demons. They latched onto my legs, and I dragged them all to the bridge spanning the abyss like a fullback trudging to the goal line to make a touchdown.

The Great Voice boomed, *"You may not cross!"*

The four demons scurried away like so many rats to sit atop their pillars, howling, spitting, gnashing, and cursing.

"Thank you." I sighed.

I stepped onto the rickety old suspension bridge with boards rotting and missing. I focused on a small light barely visible through the dense fog on the other side. I imagined the dire consequences of falling into the abyss below. I leaned over ever so slightly to peek into the dark gorge and immediately had an overwhelming desire to topple over into the chasm. Trying to resist being pulled into the dark pit stole my resolve for a moment. It was as though I was being drawn into the emptiness of my own grave. Death as an end in itself offers an irresistible, though sneaky, invitation.

I snapped back and dared not look down anymore. I gripped the ropes that slid back and forth like wet and slippery snakes. I sensed a powerful, terrible presence surrounding me, but it wasn't that of the Great Voice. Something, or rather someone, didn't want me to get to the other side.

An icy hand reached up from the dark abyss. It wrapped around my soul like a burial shroud placed over a dead man. Like a great snake coiling around its prey, waiting till all life left the body, so death could devour its victim.

Well, was I not dead? Fear slowly shadowed any light from getting to my soul, and the tiny bit of light on the other side of the dark, foul-smelling abyss dimmed to that of a tiny candle flicker.

I closed my eyes, no longer trusting my strength to combat the horde of new demons surely waiting below.

Scaly hands grabbed my arms and snatched at my legs, tearing at my flesh. The demons ranted and raved about all of my life's failures.

How could they be there? They were told not to cross.

The small voice called softly from the other side. *"You brought them with you. Your fear cleared their path."*

The grip of the cold, dead hand from the abyss strangled the very breath from me. I put the smooth agate back in my mouth and drew harder on its sweetness.

The leader of the demons bolted from underside the bridge and ran at me, clawed nails clicking on the rotting boards of the bridge. If I ran, the monster would certainly catch me. If I stood firm, it would surely devour me. Both were a deathly gamble.

I called on every spiritual being I could think of for help as the demon bore down on me. I wanted to scream, "Granny!" But all I could say was, "I believe!"

A thousand thoughts of what that could mean raced through my head like a herd of wild mustangs, each horse with a different name painted on it. The name of the stallion my mind chose to ride was Creator Never Abandons. I screamed those words at the top of my lungs.

The demon leader tripped and rolled on the bridge, stopping short of my feet like it had been shot down with a thousand arrows. Writhing in agony, the demon cried out, "You are the reason she killed herself."

I mustered every bit of what little strength I had left and screamed, "And you don't think I know that?"

The demon lifted itself from the floor of the bridge, snickering. "We will never let you forget that truth, you murderer."

"You don't have to." I believed I could defeat them by agreeing with them, but my energy drained in the bickering. I needed help. I sighed in exhausted surrender. "Forgive me, Creator, I cannot do this alone."

The old woman with long, gray hair engulfed in a multicolored, swirling agate gown spoke in a familiar, still-small voice. "You never could. But you can now."

"Granny, please help me."

The rotting boards beneath the demon collapsed with a roar. The scaly creature fell into the abyss, kicking and cursing. The others scampered back to their hiding places, laughing and threatening me.

"Thank you," I cried.

Granny was the answer to a prayer I never prayed.

I was immediately transported to the other side of the chasm, then dumped on the ground like a fish out of a basket, flopping and gasping for air.

The bridge collapsed behind me. Fresh, rough-cut wooden boards were quickly nailed up by two large hands to block the entrance. A cold shudder shook me like I had stepped over my own grave.

A signpost fell from the sky. It landed hard at my feet. I read the warning it offered, penned in my handwriting. *Point of No Return*.

I searched for God and found only myself.
I searched for myself and found only God.

—*Sufi proverb*

PART TEN

Walking into the Known Unknown

Whoever fights monsters should see to it that in the process he does not become a monster. And if you gaze long enough into an abyss, the abyss will gaze back into you.

—Friedrich Nietzsche

CHAPTER 36

Going Where I'd Not Gone Before

Courage doesn't mean you don't get afraid.
Courage means you don't let fear stop you.

—Bethany Hamilton

TIME SEEMED TO never pass in this place. No sun to rise and set. No moon and stars to come and go. No light by day, no darkness by night. Just an overcast gray firmament to dampen my fading spirits. Still, I had to go on.

I was sure I'd passed the point of no return when I sat down by the Name Tree to take the pills and drink the whiskey. Not so. I dusted myself off with no idea of where the path would lead. I followed the faint trail with no markers to a small hunting cabin similar to one I had once owned. Naomi had never gone there with me. None of the family had. I bought it as a retreat from the very people Creator had given me to love—my family—and Naomi suffered the most for it.

I quietly pushed open the cabin door. A single ray of light beamed across the room like through an old window pane on a warm afternoon. Dust particles suspended in air, floating aimlessly, suddenly became faces of souls yet to find their places. Frightening as it was, I shook off the creeping fear and reminded myself all souls are connected together in the one Great Soul because they all emanated from Creator.

But somehow I knew these souls had lost their way.

The anguish on their tiny faces mimicked Naomi's expressions on so many dark days before she left us. No matter which way I moved to get past them, they shifted to block me. Unsure of what to do, I walked into the light with them and stood still. The little dust particles, each with a version of Naomi's face, floated toward me. Hovering around me, they gently lit on me like butterflies. They smiled and cuddled my entire body. Then, they passed through my clothes and entered my body through the pores of my skin.

I shook and shuddered, gasping for air. "What is happening to me?"

The Great Voice announced matter-of-factly, "*You've taken her woes like He took yours. Your purpose is complete.*"

I felt like I had been placed into a large vise, and someone was squeezing the life from me.

I could hardly grunt out, "Where is Naomi?" I was whisked outside to stand on a muddy wagon road with deep ruts.

Granny wisped past like a puff of smoke to sit on a limb of an old dead tree, her gown waving in the breeze. She was admiring the most deliciously red apple I'd ever seen.

"May I have a bite? I'm about done in."

"No, not yet, great-grandson. The red apple of truth is only for those who are glorified on the earth by finishing the work Creator has given them to do."

I was famished and frustrated. "Have I not done that?"

"Only your purpose is complete. Your quest has just begun. Shoulder the mantle you have been given."

A large, wooden double mantle like farmers once used with oxen landed on my shoulders hard. My knees buckled as the leather straps secured the mantle to my body. I held up the larger side that bore the most weight and would do the heavy pulling. No one shouldered the other side of the mantle, typically where a young ox would have been placed for training.

The strain was more than I could bear, and I became faint. "Granny, it's too heavy."

"You are right. The weight of all that we did not do always is." Granny floated down from the tree and placed another agate rock in my mouth. The surge of energy filled my soul and strengthened my body.

"How did you know, Granny?"

"How could you not?"

I had no answer to the question, but it was clear Granny understood I did not know my own daughter as I should have.

An overloaded, medieval-style, two-wheel cart appeared behind me, holding a sign that read, "Wain of Burdens." The mantle became heavier as unseen hands hitched me to the cart. Still, no one was placed beside me to help pull.

"I can't bear the weight of the entire mantle and pull this cart at the same time by myself."

Granny stroked my face with her silky soft wrinkled hand. "Great-grandson, you are not alone. You just think you are."

"How can I do this?" I asked. "There's too much stuff loaded on it."

"You must lighten your own load before you can teach Naomi to loosen hers."

"You mean, carry her burdens until she learns to shoulder her side of the mantle?"

"You understand your purpose now." The mantle and cart disappeared, but the weight did not.

The Great Voice bellowed, *What emanates from The Great Soul will return to The Great Soul.*

I trembled as the ground quaked beneath my feet.

A rocky path appeared, and I started walking. What I had known in my soul before I ended my life flooded my mind. What I had believed since childhood was affirmed. There is but one consciousness we all share separated only by the unique identities that Creator enjoys in each of us.

Naomi and I must learn to pull the cart of burdens together. Or not at all.

I had been a fool. Only a shallow man can see others merely through his own eyes. I had done this with Naomi. I never truly knew my daughter.

I jerked and strained to pull the weight of the unseen cart as I began the journey like an Alaskan husky breaking dogsled runners frozen in the ice. With each heavy step, I was given a new piece of wisdom.

Granny whispered in my ear, "Being a creation of The Great Soul ensures that we each will blend together on that last day when the universe has finished her dance. Until then, we must continue on to the Grand Merge. That complete, we will enjoy eternal bliss as one within The Great One."

These thoughts became clear as I dragged the unseen weight of The Wain of Burdens.

I cried out, "This is a tough place to be."

Granny snickered. "Someone once said, 'Where you are is not who you are.'"

The cart became visible again for a moment. The weight of Naomi's struggles and pains filled a pack that two large hands placed on my back.

My knees buckled. I couldn't move, like a pickup truck stuck in a muddy rut.

Granny placed another living agate in my mouth as the cart disappeared, the full weight of burden now in the pack on my back. My soul came back to life. A glimmer of hope lit my path. I could go on.

Everything that is in the heavens, on earth, and under the earth is penetrated with connectedness, penetrated with relatedness.

—Hildegard of Bingen

CHAPTER 37

The Cave

I will love the light for it shows me the way, yet I will
endure the darkness because it shows me the stars.

—Og Mandino

T HAT SMALL GLIMMER of hope no longer came from
without, but from within. Warmth sustained my soul, and
I needed it.

So, there is a future in death.

With my next faltering step, darkness engulfed me. I was as lost as a
child in a cave when a tour guide turns out the lights and people can't see
a hand right in front of their faces. I fumbled forward, stumbling over
things whose identities I couldn't discern. And I didn't want to know
what they were. My eyes adjusted to the darkness as I shifted in my
backpack. I stood at the entrance of a cave with strange yet familiar
sounds emanating. What they were, I couldn't tell. Something told me I
had been here before.

A faint light, like a candle with a hand over it, offered little comfort
to the silence. I reasoned that I could only go forward, straight ahead on
a crooked path. I took a few timid steps, then picked up the pace. Or at

least increased my efforts. My legs moved sluggishly, like walking upstream in a shallow, sandy-bottomed river, heavy and laborious.

I had to keep going. Naomi was depending on me.

I squeezed through the small entrance, then stood in a large cave opening that narrowed to a smaller one. My name was chiseled on the cavern wall above the entrance. This cave was mine, and the light was dim.

As I crawled over rocks and through tight places, I vaguely remember having gone this way a long time ago.

The Great Voice shouted, *"Too long ago."*

The cave floor vibrated, and rocks fell from the ceiling and cavern walls.

"I thought you said I never got past the four pillars back at the beginning. All the footprints turned back at the point where demons sat on the pillars."

The Great Voice said, *"To the pure, all things are pure. The pure leave no footprints. All who have ever been made in Creator's image have been carried to their own cave and allowed at least once to see into their soul, as you say, back at the beginning."*

"When I was a baby? But it's been so long ago. How could I remember coming here?"

"Memory fails. Being remembers. Only the pure soul who has yet to eat of the fruit remembers this place."

"Who in the world could that be?"

No answer came.

I passed through great rooms with large and small stalactites and stalagmites pulsating like beating hearts. Some formations were diseased, wounded, broken, irregular in their rhythm. As I squeezed between them, they clutched at me this way and that, trying to stall my progress.

Tiny, whining voices sang a chorus repeatedly from flawless crystalline formations. "We are what you never became." They begged me not to go forward. Their pull was strong. They were a part of me I never knew, like seeds planted that never sprouted.

I wanted to know what I would have become but kept walking. "This is not about me."

The tiny chorus sang, "It is, more than you think. So, stay who you are. Remain safe in the no-change zone." They warned of the dangers of traveling too far into the cave.

Ragged stalagmites sassed me. "You must believe you're some kind of hero, sacrificing and denying yourself this way. We are not impressed."

"I'm not here to impress."

Jagged stalactites cursed me for my bravery. "Even the best of the best fall to the ground."

I mustered up the courage to keep moving past them. I didn't know where I was, but I knew the way. I'd never been this far in before, but it was a familiar path. Too familiar.

I neared the end as the columns beat faster and faster, like they would explode any second. Large pieces of rock dropped to block my path, each with a phrase or word quickly painted on it by an unseen hand as they landed on the floor of the cave. Painted in bright red were conflicts and hindrances to righteous living, toxic relationships, and poor decisions I'd made in life. The very things I couldn't deal with, or rather, wouldn't. These barriers were the same that had caused Naomi to be here. The paint dripped to the floor of the cave like blood.

Without warning, formations shattered like the Philistine temple Samson brought down. The ceiling crumbled.

I frantically looked for a way out but saw none. There was no escaping this.

A small, blue ball of light appeared. Granny's face was at the center.

I chased after the blue light, scampering over broken debris, navigating collapsing stalactites and stalagmites. The last fragment to fall, barely missing me, had a warning etched into it.

You Will Surely Fail!

A small crevice opened in the wall, and I ducked in as a mighty roar of rock collapsed behind me. I was sealed in a cold, dark crack in the earth.

The blue light stopped, then Granny spoke. "I can offer no guidance to an empath run amuck. This you must do on your own with the Great Alone. Follow the path, and the load you carry may be lightened." The blue ball of light with Granny's face in the center vanished.

The Great Voice echoed from far away. *"Come!"*

Do not fight to expel the darkness from the chamber of your soul. Open a tiny aperture for light to enter, and the darkness will disappear.

—St. Porphyrios

CHAPTER 38
Walking Around in My Own Soul

*Whenever you are alone, remind yourself that God has sent
everyone else away so that there is only you and Him.*

—Rumi

I CRAWLED THROUGH the small opening into an ancient tomb like one in Israel I'd seen in a book. A large, round stone had been removed. Strange, it could only be moved from the inside. I half fell from the tiny tunnel onto the floor. Getting up, I bumped my head against the low ceiling. There was no light inside, but I could see perfectly. A thousand small caverns trailing off into a thousand different directions left me wondering where to start. They all seemed so familiar.

Too familiar.

I took one step, and all that was hidden there flooded my soul with a thousand memories of everything that had gone wrong in my life. I dropped to my knees like an anvil had been tied around my neck.

I didn't want to look. Didn't want to know. Surely didn't want to confess.

Besides feeling the weight of all that waited in those dark spaces, sharp objects cut my knees. Black blood trickled across the cave floor, viscous and foul smelling. Mine.

A tiny light appeared, again like the faint flicker of a small candle. And though it did not light up the vast cavern system, I was immediately, though uncomfortably, drawn to it. I sensed a great presence in what appeared to be an old oil clay lamp from biblical days, floating around like it was studying me. Suddenly, it moved fast as lightning to position itself in front of my face.

I had the irresistible urge to remove my shoes. I'd never experienced this feeling before. Overwhelming wonder, matchless awe, and power beyond measure. The weight of the burden I'd been carrying fell from my neck, and I dropped facedown to the ground.

The stench of my ragged clothes made me spew dark and rotting vomit on the cave floor. I wiped my mouth, then a hand pulled me to my feet. The gap between me and the Presence of the One Who Held Out His Hand was as wide as the universe itself but as close as the atoms that formed my body. I stood before the Being like a criminal before a judge about to pass sentence for the worst crimes of humanity. I knew my sentence and closed my eyes while waiting for my punishment to be announced.

Two hands landed on my shoulders like a king blessing his son to succeed him. A face that was no face formed before me. It resembled steam rising from a tea kettle but made no sound.

"Walk these rooms. It will take time, for there are many."

Fear weakened the bit of resolve I had left, and my legs gave way beneath me.

The two hands caught me and stood me back up. *"There is no need for that. I am here. I will walk with you as light is brought to every crack and crevice in this dark place of your soul. My Light chases fear back to the one who brought it here. Know that I will not be surprised by anything I see, for I see all. I know you, I love you, and I will heal you. Just walk around in your own soul with me."*

I never took a step yet traveled to every dark corner of my soul. The cave floor, though flat, was rough with potholes of old wounds and pain.

The ground was littered with the broken glass of shattered relationships. Sharp rocks and debris of bad decisions tripped me. I fell on old boards filled with the rusty nails of returning to the same wicked comforts that never brought relief. But the spiritual wounds healed instantly.

And I confessed. "Everything here belongs to me and no one else."

As I returned to my body, I realized the Great Presence still remained, having never left my side. I reached for help.

"*I cannot. If I do, then you will not have done this by your own choosing.*"

"Choose what?"

"*To remember and not forget. The Great Serpent only holds the power you give him.*"

Words of the Great Presence echoed through the caverns. Then, I heard them no more. I was alone.

Or so I thought.

All the darkness in the world cannot extinguish the light of a single candle.

—*St. Francis of Assisi*

CHAPTER 39

The Great Serpent

The Devil doesn't come from the Hell below us.
No, the Devil comes from the Hell within us.

—the author

A LARGE SERPENT with eyes covering its entire body, except for the top of his head, slithered along a ledge about six feet up on the cavern wall. Its tongue flicked left and right, searching for its prey. The walls closed in just enough that the snake with many eyes could tickle my ear with its slimy tongue. Its breath reminded me of a rotten decomposing body, sweet but foul.

"I know everything that goes on in here, heh, heh, heh." The Great Serpent's chuckle dripped with malice.

I turned to the Great Presence, but no one was there. I steadied myself for the coming bite that would end my quest and seal my fate.

"Oh, don't worry. I don't bite. I just wait for that perfect moment when I can swallow you whole. It's painless. Well, at least until you get deep inside. But hey, you won't be alone in there like you used to feel so often. Like you do now. You have many friends in my fiery lake."

"I know who you are, Great Serpent."

"How could that be?"

"You've bitten me before."

"Good, then. No need for useless and unnecessary introductions."

"You should know I've never felt alone. Not even now."

"Good, good. Just keep telling yourself that. I love lies. They are my specialty and make me feel all warm and cuddly inside, like a good meal in my belly. Some have even called me the father of them all. Lies, that is. What a compliment. I may not be all they say I am, but I can certainly help you become the greatest liar of them all. Lord knows, you've told one or two. You can even have my title. How about it? That way, at least you can still be the father of something since you... well, you know. You weren't the good father to your daughter you believed yourself to be."

I winced at the charge against me. That's one lie the Accuser had not fathered. I did.

"Don't worry, friend. Your secrets are always safe with me."

I cringed at the thought of all the lies I'd told, all the wicked things I'd covered up, and the sins I'd allowed myself, believing I deserved special treatment for being such a notable minister to the poor. Another lie I had fathered and believed.

I walked a little farther to where the path split.

The Great Serpent followed along on the ledge, close to my head. One trail was hardly used, while the other was well-worn.

The Great Serpent sneaked close, tickling my ear again. "Isn't it great that you can choose an easier way?"

I trembled at the thought of going where I had to go. Fear seized my heart, for I knew what lay ahead.

The tickling tongue soothed my fears.

"It's been too long since I've gone down this road."

The Great Serpent coiled around me, offering familiar comfort. "You don't have to go that way right now. Wait a bit. We'll return in a little while. You have pleeennnty of time, my friend. Didn't Creator say a thousand years is as a day, and a day is as a thousand years?"

"Yes, but don't I—"

"What? Have a choice?"

"I do have a choice, don't I?"

"Of course you do, old friend."

My insides danced, and my head swooned. My every desire—good and not so good—pulled me toward the well-worn path. I dug in my heels but couldn't stop, like watching a video with the remote that had no stop button.

"No!"

I'd been down the wrong road that led to nowhere too many times.

"Oh, no need for that. I promise to bring you back to this very spot anytime you please. I understand you feel it necessary to face all the wrong things you've done, but you have all the time in the world for that."

"You do know I'm dead, don't you?"

"How can that be? You never really die, don't you know? Are you not talking and walking with me?"

For a second, I thought, *That does makes sense.*

"Death is simply an illusion that's really no problem at all. But one thing's for sure, you won't know what you're missing if you don't come with me. I've upgraded The Palace of Ten Thousand Delights and have another ten thousand delights especially reserved for you. Come with me, and you'll never be alone again. My palace always draws the finest people."

I studied the less-used trail, overgrown with undesirable flora and littered with debris like a tornado had passed through long ago. No one had traveled that path in a very long time. I had no tools to clear the way. I looked back at the well-lit, red-carpeted staircase descending into a beautiful crimson valley from which the sound of a great party emanated. I liked the idea of never having to think about my wrongs or face those pains ever again.

The coils of the Great Serpent tightened about me like the warmth of my mother's arms when she rocked me to sleep as a child. "What does it matter? Put off your quest for just a little while. Relax. You've done enough for today. Tomorrow, you can start your journey again. Soul, take thine ease…." The Great Serpent slithered around me, circling faster and faster.

I was very much alert, but my strength to resist weakened. My thoughts spun like a child's toy top in my head. I was losing control and just wanted to give in. "I could take just a short break from all of this, couldn't I?"

The Great Serpent slowed its revolutions but tightened its cooling coils. "You deserve a little rest and recreation. After all, you did make the greatest of sacrifices. What more could be asked of such a loyal servant, hmmm?"

There's that word again. *Deserve*. Applying it to me has never felt right.

"You don't want to miss out soaking in the soothing ocher waters of Brimstone Lake, where we'll all soon swim. I acquired beachfront property a few millennia ago and am still expanding to accommodate new arrivals every day. I have a room reserved in your name, the Golden Street Suite, with a door made of the finest pearl. It leads to the greatest of pleasurable joys. You have visited several times before. Don't you remember?"

A faint memory jogged of a recurring dream I'd had some years back. The vision came at my weakest moments, when I did things I knew to be wrong against those whom I loved—Creator, my family, but mostly myself. I was so ashamed to know this place so well. The beautiful palace, fiery lake, and every sinful pleasure one could ever imagine, just for the asking. I remembered waking to how real the dream had seemed. There was a part of me that held this place dear to my soul. To escape this place of surrender to pleasure, I would have to endure a painful change because Creator's purifying fire burns much hotter than the flames of the Lake of Fire. Otherwise, I wouldn't keep returning to the same place where I created more pain for myself.

"No dream here, my friend. In my palace, you will have all the comforts of the grandest casino. The lights are always on, you can eat to your heart's desire, and you can play the games twenty-four-seven because your money is no good here. You can have as many or as much of, well, whatever it is you enjoy the most. We have pulled out all the stops, spared no expense, and your secrets are safe with me. But you already know that. In my palace, you don't have to ever think about anything you don't want to. We'll talk about the minor details later. You have plenty of time. Now, come with me and enjoy yourself. Set yourself free in the Halls of No Limits. You have earned the right to rest and enjoy. You deserve it."

I stepped onto the well-worn path, and the Great Serpent relaxed its grip. I was free to choose, but part of me held back.

A wisp of a whisper called from a place that seemed far removed from where I stood. I cupped my hand over my ear, straining to hear the still small voice.

"I will never leave nor forsake you," echoed like through an endless canyon.

The Great Serpent hissed and wrapped around me again, tightening its grip.

I couldn't breathe. I tried to break free but was unable. I sucked in what I believed to be my last breath, then called out, "I need help."

A bright flash of lightning peeled away the Great Serpent's grip on me. It screamed and snapped at the blurry Being with a Flaming Sword clothed in shining armor. The figure, man or woman, I couldn't tell, battled with such speed and accuracy that the Great Serpent was unable to fend off the deadly strikes. Finally, the Armored Warrior captured the Great Serpent, who writhed in its bloody wounds and bared its fangs at the One Who Pinned Him to the Ground with the Flaming Sword.

The Armored Warrior looked to the heavens. "Now, may I?"

The Great Voice thundered, *"His time is not yet."*

The Warrior released the Great Serpent.

Fiery cinders fell from its skin as it descended the red staircase to The Palace of Ten Thousand Delights. What I had taken to be a grand party became the screams of souls who still thought they had made the right choice.

The Great Serpent turned and grinned. "I'll see you again. It's already been planned." He disappeared into the fiery cauldron of tortured souls receiving the wrath of a defeated master.

I shuddered so hard my bones rattled. Cinders that had attached themselves to my skin in the battle between the Great Serpent and the Armored Being of Light fell from my body. I drew in a long, deep breath and sighed in relief.

I kneeled to rest and reflect.

———————————————

Be careful of whose voice you hear and wise to whom you listen. Even Satan speaks a little truth. I know. I've heard him.

—the author

CHAPTER 40

New Day Dawning

The Psalmist wrote, "Joy comes with the morning."
He never promised it would last.

—the author

A BLINDING LIGHT refracted through a rainbow, filling the cavern like the new morning sun breaking over a hill.

"My goodness, would you look at that?"

"It's a promise just for you, great-grandson."

"Granny, it's just like the verse you used to quote. His mercies are new every morning. Therefore, I will hope in my Creator."

"You now have the right foundation for your quest." Granny faded into the smooth, polished agate floor.

"*There is no place I will not go with you,*" the Great Voice spoke with authority.

"How did I become so conflicted? I've always known the right path to take."

Creator said nothing.

I felt bewildered. But then again, there's no need for pats on the head for doing what you always knew was right.

The Armored Warrior with the Flaming Sword stood guard at the entrance to the Great Serpent's lair and stepped forward. "Make the choice you have always known to be true." The angel of light stepped back and sheathed the flaming sword.

"I can't do this by myself. It's not in me."

"You have no idea what's in you, my son," the Great Voice chided.

The Armored Warrior with the Flaming Sword stepped up again. "If you could but see with Eyes of True Reality, you would know The One Within is so great that the enemies who wage war against your purpose are as rodents at your feet. Trust your true eyes."

I dusted off the remaining cinders and turned to the path less walked. "All right, then. I'll go and face it. I'll face me."

The Armored Warrior with the Flaming Sword rolled the stone back into place. He returned to his post guarding the path to the Great Serpent's lair.

"You are now safe and protected." The Great Voice sounded relieved.

The dazzling lights of The Palace of Ten Thousand Delights went dark, and the screams of lost souls faded.

"Now I can be everywhere present with you, my son," the Great Voice affirmed.

Curtains resembling vertical ocean waves traveling up and down at rapid speed dropped from the sky.

Something moved, like a small scared rabbit dashing from behind a bush.

I chased after it into the watery curtains with all the speed I could muster.

I didn't know why.

My heart just said, Do it.

It was simply the right thing to do.

I must totally disown my self-rejecting voice and claim the truth that God does indeed want to embrace me.

—Henri Nouwen

PART ELEVEN

The Descent

The path of descent is the path of transformation.
Darkness, failure, relapse, death, and woundedness
are our primary teachers, rather than ideas or doctrines.

—Richard Rohr

CHAPTER 41

The Three Trials of My Descent

When I let go of who I am, I become what I might be.

—Lao Tzu

As I RACED through one sheer curtain to the next, a pale light slowly became brighter. I strained to keep my eyes trained on it. If I didn't, it'd be like a leaf swept away in a gust of watery wind. The change was so subtle, I could hardly tell the difference with each step. The darkness diminished, and the curtains opened, but only just enough to reveal a small person balled up and shaking.

A small, blonde girl with blue eyes and a distorted face of pain looked up. She wore a ragged sack dress, her hair disheveled and makeup streaming down her teary cheeks. She shivered, not from the cold, for she had been huddling near a blazing furnace. She couldn't have known the flames were evil spirits grasping to pull her in until she saw me. Her eyes widened, and she scampered away, frightened.

Naomi.

She didn't know me. I saw it in her eyes. And so I cried. Bitterly.

I wandered aimlessly through a thousand warm curtains that became violent blasts of frigid air with each new step. I rubbed my shoulders and stomped my feet to shake off the cold.

Hard as I tried, I could not catch up with Naomi. I was happy that at least I'd seen my daughter. She didn't look like herself. But who else could it be but her? I didn't care. I'd take her in any condition.

I ran faster and finally caught another glimpse of her.

Why can't I catch her? She must still be unsure about me.

Naomi stayed just beyond my reach. Something wouldn't allow me to step into the same space between curtains with her. She was always just one curtain ahead of me.

"You cannot catch her until she acknowledges you as her father," the Great Voice boomed.

Time passed. How much, I don't know, but I kept racing through more curtains, each becoming a little brighter. I finally caught up with her. Rather, she stopped with a start. Still as a statue, she tilted her head, studying me. Still uncertain as to who I was. At least she'd stopped running.

Her eyes searched like that of a blind person who believed someone was in the room with her but wasn't sure.

Naomi didn't recognize me. The realization felt like my heart had fallen out of my chest and hit the ground hard.

I picked myself up emotionally and took one step. The ground before me shook, and a crack formed in the earth about a foot wide. I took another step. It widened to six feet, then another and another, until Naomi stood across a great chasm some hundred yards between us, the bottom of which I could not see.

I wanted to rush and hold her, to tell her how much I loved her. A part of me became hopeless because of the great distance between us. The rest of me wanted to trust that I could walk on air and go to her on the other side.

If I can just get a good running start....

Just before I made the leap that surely would have been the end of me and my quest, I saw a path that led to the bottom of the shadowy gorge.

I was truly afraid for the first time in my life. Not of punishment or danger. Dad had beaten the fear of punishment out of me when I was growing up. So much so that facing danger was like a drug-induced high for me. No, this fear sent chills up and down my spine like an army of little ice men marching continuously back and forth. It wasn't about bodily harm. This fear was about failing, and I knew where it came from—my failure as a father handed down to me from my failed father, and in turn, his from his failed father.

A sack of rocks bearing the weight of the generations was added to the burden I carried for Naomi on my back. The load was so heavy. It was too much. I dropped to my knees.

The Great Voice spoke, shaking the ground on which I kneeled. *"You must descend in order to ascend. You must leave It in the pit."*

"What is It?" I cried out.

As expected, I received no answer.

The descending path resembled a scene out of Dante's Inferno, but I figured it was going to be much worse. Noises that would make the bravest man shudder and the meanest man wilt erupted from the darkness. I felt both.

I could see Naomi across the great divide that separated us. She searched the skies like she was trying to find the sun. Rainbow butterflies fluttered all around her but couldn't light. Those that tried burst into a thousand sparkles. Something must change for them to land safely.

Granny laid her hand on my shoulder, then pulled me up. She kissed the back of my neck. "This, great-grandson, will not be easy."

"What are those butterflies?"

"All the gifts and talents Naomi once possessed of which you had no knowledge. They are rapidly diminishing by the power of the one who rules the pit."

I turned, but Granny was gone. I looked around, then up. "How could I have not known?"

The Great Voice said, *"You did not care to know."*

Naomi stepped out onto the ledge, lifted her arms to the sky, then dove from her side of the gorge into the pit below.

I screamed, "No!"

She took her own life.

I rushed to the edge, ready to dive after her, but a large hand caught me before I plunged from the ledge.

"I have to save her, can't you see?"

"We shall see," the Great Voice said matter-of-factly.

"Why won't you let me go after her?"

"Doing things your way? I don't think so."

"Are you really my Creator? How do I know you're not that big snake come to deceive and defeat me?"

"You don't. You must decide whose voice it is that you hear."

"How can I know?"

"When you remove 'I' from your conversation."

"I, my, me?"

"Exactly."

"Will Naomi's butterflies be returned to her?"

"They will not befriend her until she knows her name, nor will she survive unless she finds It."

"What is *It*?"

Of course, there was no answer. I didn't even try to find out where the voice was coming from.

Granny whispered, "In the isolation of the chrysalis do the butterfly's wings mature."

I wasn't sure exactly what she meant, but I had an idea. So, like they say in the Good Book, I girded up my loins and took my first step into the abyss where I would help set Naomi free.

I would have to change. It was, as they say, about damn time.

Love springs from awareness.

—*Anthony de Mello*

CHAPTER 42

An Unexpected but Familiar Guide, Again

The dead are not distant or absent... they continue to be near us and part of the healing of grief is the refinement of our hearts whereby we come to sense their loving nearness... When we ourselves enter the eternal world and come to see our lives on earth in full view, we may be surprised at the immense assistance and support with which our departed loved ones have accompanied every moment of our lives.

—John O'Donohue (1956-2008)

THE ABYSS ONLY offered two steps leading downward. After that, darkness. Life has been that way, never able to see far enough ahead to know when you'll trip and fall. When I fell in life, as I did so many times, there was little to stop me from plunging headlong into places I never planned or wanted to go. When I arrived, I wish I hadn't. By then though, it was too late. And now? This promised to be the greater plunge.

My soul retreated a bit. My body pushed on.

I inched my way closer to the path of my descent. The first full step would be the hardest. I was afraid of what it might lead to. When I shifted the sack of rocks on my shoulders and the burden pack I carried for Naomi, a scaly, clawed hand snatched my feet out from underneath me. A demon yanked the spiritual rug right out from under me.

I tumbled end over end until I landed on a ledge hardly the width of my shoulders. Cuts and bruises covered my body. I bled like a slaughtered animal. I couldn't move, couldn't breathe. The darkness was thick enough to cut with a knife.

Like serpents slithering out of their resting places in the clefts and cracks of the wall next to me, demons with shiny claws and fangs crept forward like a snake charming a mouse, never taking their eyes from me. Lean and hungry, they drooled like rabid dogs, clearly planning to make me their next meal.

A deep, gravelly voice heckled me from the bottom of the abyss. Fear stole my soul, and I caved. I scrambled back up the path I had just rolled down as quickly as my hands and feet would take me. With each rock kicked loose or dead root yanked free, I slid farther down into the pit. Then, I figured it out.

As each rock tumbled and each root fell to the side, I had to acknowledge what must be torn from my soul—hurt, anger, hate, abuse, violence. The list kept growing.

Will I ever get there? Will I make it?

I clawed at the stinking mud like crawling over a thousand dead bodies, all of which were mine. The stench of my wrongs was almost more than I could bear. I called out the names of my hindrances. One by one, the rocks of faults so deeply embedded in the mud of my dead self broke loose, then rolled into the abyss. I searched my soul and racked my brain to confess everything I could remember. Part of me did not want to for fear I wouldn't be accepted by Naomi if she heard my true confessions. But I did it anyway, and my burden immediately became lighter. The sack of rocks on my back had emptied, and I vowed to never pick them up again.

So, fear can be useful.

Exhausted, I crawled up the hill at a painstakingly slow pace. I pulled myself up to the edge, barely hanging on, my fingers digging deep into the slippery clayish ground. I remembered Naomi helping me up the muddy slope the day we found the Name Tree so many years ago, and I her. But she wasn't there to help me, just like I wasn't there to help her when she needed me most. I rested in a strain, but soon my hold weakened. I couldn't pull myself out.

Just as I started to slide back into the abyss, a small, withered hand reached for mine. The lightest touch of her fingertips lifted me up without effort, then she set me down on my feet with my back to the gorge.

A very old but familiar woman with a concerned face sat on a stool by the wall. Her hair shimmered like the icicles Naomi and I had placed on our Christmas tree one year. She wore a glowing, translucent robe of agate.

I cleared bits of stinking mud from my eyes. "Granny? That you again?"

"Don't you know?"

"It's difficult to know who to trust in this place."

"Therein lies the problem."

"And why would that be?" Frustrated, I kicked at a rock.

"You must know your true self to trust another."

"Can't know Creator until I know myself, that it? Yeah, I read that somewhere."

"You speak truth your own ears need to hear and your soul needs to feed upon."

"If it is you, why do you change so often?"

She kept rolling something around in her hand. "It is Creator's way— always creating, ever-renewing. You should try it sometime."

Then, in an instant, Granny became the epitome of beauty and perfection, flawless and completeness, youth at its very best—bright red hair, flashing green eyes, and a sassy temperament that came with her rich Irish heritage.

I gasped as her fierce green gaze drilled into me. "Granny, you're... you're so beautiful. Where did that come from?"

"You must learn to listen, great-grandson." Her voice changed from momentary anger to that of the small trickling stream by the Name Tree.

"Forgive me, I'm trying. It's so much to take in, and...."

"This beauty only comes from the place you have always known to be true and real, where all things wonderfully beautiful begin in the mind of God."

"Where did you hear those words?"

"Why, from you, great-grandson. They are yours. Don't you remember?"

"I do. I wrote them after my trip with Naomi when we found the Name Tree."

"The preacher must listen to his own words and then believe."

"What do you mean?"

"You must see Naomi as truly she was, before she was, in the mind of Creator."

"Then I do believe."

"We'll see. One thing must happen to open your eyes that you might see your daughter, in all her beauty and perfection, as flawless and complete."

"What is that?"

"Light up the darkness within yourself before you attempt to shine into another's soul."

The ledge crumbled beneath my feet, but I caught myself just in time. Hanging by a thread of bloody fingertips, I didn't have the power to pull myself up. The little strength I had left after trying to get out of the chasm of horrors was gone. My fingers slipped, and the demons snickered as they anxiously awaited my fall into the shadows of the path below.

"Granny, will you help me?"

She grabbed my shirt at the shoulders with one hand. With one pull, her wrinkled and feeble arm yanked me up with the might of a lion. She spun me around, then kissed me on the back of the neck again like she did when I was a young boy. "That's all you had to say, great-grandson. I've waited a long time for you to ask that question."

My clothes, torn and ragged, became shifting snakes with an accusatory word written on each. They hissed and slithered, coiling around my body, ready to strike. I shuddered uncontrollably. Each had a wicked human face with a fanged smile waiting its turn to take a bite of my flesh. I tried to jump back, but where was I to go? If I brushed them off, they would bite me.

The list of words describing me kept growing as the serpents tightened their grip. I recognized every word glowing a ghoulish green— liar, thief, cheat, abuser, selfish, violent, blamer, indifferent, enraged, glory-seeking. When one snake disappeared behind my back, three more took its place.

"Are these my clothes?"

"You have worn them well. Like they say, the clothes do make the man." Sharp, needle-like pains stabbed me all over.

"They're biting me!" I brushed and pulled at them as fast as I could, but they became stronger, and blood covered my hands.

"No worries, child. They've already bitten you many, many times. And though their venom is quite lethal, you are somewhat immune."

"Somewhat immune? Am I that bad? Am I going to die here?"

"Oh, no, great-grandson. The Great Serpent still keeps his promise that you will surely not die."

I scratched and clawed at the snakes. "I want them off! How do I get them off, Granny?"

"Hmmm, do you not know the answer?"

"No, I don't." The harder I worked, the faster the snakes moved about my body.

Granny seemed unconcerned at my growing plight. "Wonder of wonders, oh I wonder, what could possibly cover a multitude of painful wrongs?"

My head dropped like a kid caught with his hand in the cookie jar. The snakes stopped cold to listen. I knew the answer all too well. It was a memory verse I'd learned when I won a red leather Bible in a church contest as a kid. Granny had taught me the very same words.

"I know. Love covers a multitude of sins."

"Do you really know?"

"Yes. Yes, I do. Now."

Granny's flowing robe burst into a thousand sparkling lights blinking like a Christmas tree. They dimmed a little, and I could see her face had returned to the one I grew up with.

I held up my hands. "What about these?" My arms dripped blood from the fang wounds.

The Great Serpent snickered. His deep, gravelly voice came from the abyss. "Your hands are now fully prepared to do the work for which you have become so adept—loving yourself." The snakes disappeared into my ragged clothes.

Granny held out her small hand like she was offering me a gift. "Be open and honest within yourself, and your hands will heal to do the right and best things."

"But I've confessed to Creator everything I can think of. I'd be glad to tell you things you probably already know."

"That won't do. You must enter the Holy of Holies where the Great Alone lives. You must confess in the deepest of all places to hear The Great Voice. Only there will the truth you seek be revealed."

I didn't like the sound of that. "Isn't that God?"

"No."

"Then who?"

Her eyes became purple amethyst stones blinking on and off like a traffic caution light. "You've known the other side was just beyond the thin veil. I taught you that long ago in preparation for this very moment. You found thin spots as you wandered the hills and lived for days on the river. The agates I left there for you were glimpses of what you now see. You must continue on this path of believing who you are as Creator has purposed you—one who feels the souls of all humankind.

You'll find *It* laying on the Mercy Seat of your own making. Once you accept the truth of that gift and not flee from it, you will know your place in the universe."

"But Granny, there's only one Mercy Seat in the Holy of Holies, where Creator sits."

"Creator did not build the mercy seat I send you to, great-grandson."

"Then who did?"

"You. You built the seat of your own mercies for those sins you allowed yourself and refused to face."

My heart dropped like a rock in a great lake, lost. I didn't know what to do next.

"Take this." Granny handed me an agate like so many I'd found along the Mississippi River. It was much more beautiful than the ones she'd previously given me. It was polished smooth, and the wavy lines moved and shifted in a thousand different patterns with a thousand different colors.

"Thank you."

"Hold it close to the secret place of your soul, and it will always give you light."

"I can't go alone, Granny."

"You don't have to."

"How can I find Naomi?"

"Shed all that lay between the two of you, and *Pleasantness* will be yours."

"I'm not sure I have the strength."

"You never did."

"Then where will I get the strength?"

"Ah, from the One Who Always Remains."

"Where can I find the One Who Always Remains?"

"In the place where faith and hope no longer sustain the soul."

Then, it hit me like a ton of bricks. "I've never loved myself?"

"Now you understand."

"How could I have ever loved Naomi if I never loved myself?"

"That is the question. She can never be free until you free yourself."

In a fading mist the color of her amethyst eyes, Granny melted into the wall.

Our sins are nothing but a grain of sand along the great mountain of the mercy of God.

—St. John Vianney

Now is where love breathes.

—Rumi

CHAPTER 43

The Shedding

Just as a snake sheds its skin,
we must shed our past over and over again.

—Buddha

I CLINCHED THE agate rock in my hand and held it to my chest. A chorus of strange and horrifying noises erupted like myriad katydids calling in the trees on a sultry southern night.

I considered my choices.

"There's only one." The Great Voice spoke like thunder. *"To free yourself, you must love yourself. What you now understand must happen. What must happen is for you to do. Only you."*

I stood at the top of the abyss, gazing down the path of darkness, strengthening my resolve. The more I loosened the bindings of my own soul's making—hate, anger, grudge-holding—the weaker the grip of the snakes became. Soon, the words written on their skins faded, and they began to drop off. One by one, they fell, becoming dust on the ground, then blowing away in a subtle breeze.

Granny reappeared in a blinding blue light. "You must shed the snakeskins of your own making to be truly bare and honest before Creator."

"It is love, not power. Isn't it, Granny?"

She nodded.

I tried to remember that old verse on a card she once sent in the mail along with a birthday gift. My mother made me put it up on my bathroom mirror so I would read it every morning. At the time, I resented it being forced upon me. I didn't feel that any longer.

"What were those words again? Patient, kind, keeps no record of wrongs, and…."

Granny smiled. "That's the one. Keeping your own list of wrongs done against yourself feeds the others. Get rid of that one first."

I tried to remember everyone who had done me wrong. I called out each name, then spoke words of forgiveness for them and words of apology for me for holding grudges against them.

"You are almost ready."

I took one step, then the voices of a thousand demons screamed like an ancient barbaric army shouting wild encouragement to each other before a great attack. I looked back at Granny, who stood solid as the rock in my hand.

She smiled. "There is no other way."

I readied myself to war against the horde of the Great Serpent. I expected to receive a suit of armor for the coming battle, maybe even a horse and a flaming sword. Nothing appeared.

A frigid breeze sucked the warmth out of my soul. It ripped off my garments like the skin had been snatched from my body. Everything I had previously clothed myself with to hide the shame of my wrongdoing vanished in a puff of ashy smoke.

Totally exposed, it wasn't my naked body that bothered me. Stripped of the trappings of my former world, everything I had put my trust in had disappeared. What little power I thought I once had was gone. There was never any power in those things except of my own making. I had come to believe my own lies and gotten pretty good at hiding my weaknesses.

From the ashes of my clothes that fell to the ground, more snakes of my making appeared at my feet, wrapping around my legs to hold me in place. They no longer hid in the shadows like when I looked for copperheads in the hollow where Naomi and I found the Name Tree. No, these serpents had no fear of exposing my deepest, most secret sinful thoughts. I didn't want to look at myself. Each snake carried a particular wrong that I had refused to face. These things held me back from surrendering completely to what would cover over a multitude of wrongs—love.

Great and painful sores erupted where the serpents had once clung to my body. Tiny newborn snakes hatched just under my skin, then poured out of new gashes like their den was on fire. So painful were the wounds, I fell to the ground and screamed in agony.

The tiny snakes burst into uncontrollable laughter. They all lined up like a children's chorus, their beady little eyes hungrily fixed on me. They sang to the tune of my favorite children's song, *"Frere Jacques."*

"We will sta-ay, we will sta-ay. Yes, we will, yes, we will. We will never leave you, we will never leave you. No, we won't. No, we won't."

"Even the smallest ones have the look of the Great Serpent," I cried.

Suddenly, the demon chorus fell silent. The tiny serpents raced past the older snakes still at my feet, slithering down the path into the darkness I would soon travel. Certainly they went to set a trap.

My wounds slowly healed, and my flesh returned to normal. I examined my body for any lingering snakes or festering sores, but there were none. I stood, alone and bare, before the Universe—no plan, no weapon, and no direction to travel except forward and downward into a pit reserved for me. I had nothing. I realized it wasn't important if I survived this quest. It only mattered that I completely trusted the One who would help me set Naomi free.

For a brief moment, my nakedness didn't embarrass or unsettle me. I remembered reading about an old mystic who practiced his spirituality living unclothed in the desert for years. He penned centuries ago, "To truly face yourself, you must cast off all you hold dear that hinders spiritual progress. You must see all that is there. All is none, and none is all."

I shook the vipers from my legs and feet, stepped out of the pile of writhing putrid madness, then screamed, "No more!"

My body strengthened. My skin became pure and fresh, without blemish, like a newborn babe's. I had the energy to run and never stop. I'd never felt so good and sharp-minded in all my life as I did in that moment. I had been regenerated from head to toe, inside and out.

A large hand set a body-length mirror in front of me. For a second, I caught a brief glimpse of a once diseased, rotting corpse with my face writhing in pain and agony. A fierce gust of wind blew scales from my eyes. That was the old me. For the first time, I saw the true me. The me before I gave myself away. I didn't recognize myself.

The Great Voice announced in a pleasingly proud tone, *"You are as you were before you were born, in My Creative Mind."*

The words floated into my mouth and tasted like the purest honey. They filled me to brimming over with a power that was never mine.

The lightest touch, like the wing of a butterfly, brushed my shoulder. "I have witnessed all." Granny went and stood by the stone wall. "Now, you are ready."

I peeked into the abyss of writhing demonic serpents, never more unsure about attempting to do anything in all my life, but also never more unafraid to take the first step. I held the agate Granny had given me close to my chest.

She leaned forward and puffed from her nostrils an indescribably sweet, fragrant cloud that smelled like the sassafras tea she used to make.

I breathed deeply as the mist engulfed me. "I feel so new and clean, Granny."

"The Spirit has that effect against all foes of Creator. What's inside cannot remain the same, great-grandson."

The Great Voice boomed again. *"Your fear has been entirely of your own making."*

Granny smiled proudly and touched the agate with her aged and crooked finger. The stone glowed, and the markings swirled with the power of the Universe.

My resolve strengthened as my heart warmed. I looked straight into the abyss of my inner person unflinchingly, and the demons on the path below fell silent.

Then, I took my first step to find Naomi.

Yesterday is gone. Tomorrow has not yet come.
We have only today. Let us begin.

—*Mother Teresa*

CHAPTER 44

The First Descent

Rebuilding begins with the stones of ruin.

—the author

C UPPING MY HANDS to hide the light of the agate stone, I sneaked down the darkening path, thinking if I was quiet enough, maybe the demons would forget I was there. I should have known better. I did know better. I'd been trying to sneak past them most of my life.

Without warning, clawed hands stretched and slashed, ripping my exposed skin. I opened my hands, and the agate rock's light drove the wicked creatures back into their cracks and crevices. Their red, flaming, beady eyes glared at me like wolves stalking a lamb. I held the light higher, and they remained in their lairs, cursing and gnashing their teeth.

The path flattened a bit, and a grayish sun rose as I passed through a rusty wrought iron fence gate surrounding an old cemetery. An old man sat in a homemade straight-back chair, chewing tobacco with a moonshine jug at his feet. He held an old revolver in his hand, snapping the trigger and grinning like he hit everything he shot at. Though I'd never met this man, I knew him from old family pictures.

"Great-grandpa?"

He didn't turn to acknowledge me. He just stared straight ahead, watching something intently, then leaned forward and spat a long stream of tobacco that landed in a brass spittoon with a ding. "One and the same, boy." He pulled up the moonshine jug and took a swig.

"You don't know me but, I am—"

"I know exactly who you are. Don't you think an old man knows his kin? I've been watching you from afar for a long time."

"Why are you here?"

"Not the right question, great-grandson."

"Then what is the right question?"

"How do you want to go on from here?" He turned and smiled. "Now, that's the right question." Great-grandpa raised the pistol and fired three quick snaps at some unseen target. "Got him right between the eyes, heh, heh! Still the best shot in the county." He blew invisible smoke from the end of the pistol barrel.

I had to know. "You must have a reason for being here."

"I do."

"Can I ask what it is?"

"Sure, same as you. I'm just trying to find redemption."

"Have you found it yet?"

"Nope. I'm too damn stubborn, I reckon."

"Why?"

He pointed to a screen that looked like it would've been in an old 1920s movie house. "I can't take my eyes off that moving picture show about things that seem so familiar to me. The actor in the story looks a lot like me. He's dressed like me, but I don't remember doing any of those things. But I like what I see. Can you explain that?"

"No, sir. I can't."

"Well, I don't know what else to do except sit here and keep watching this picture show. I just wish I could hear what's being said. Maybe somebody smart will invent movies one day that'll talk instead of just playing useless music. But that's all right. I got my tobacco and moonshine to keep me company, and they don't talk back. What else could a man need? Well, I do have my pistol. A man's got to have at least a little entertainment now and then. That dang music does bother the hell out of me, though." He took three more shots at the screen. It sounded like a kid's cap gun going off.

I studied the black and white film on the large screen before us. The music, definitely from the 1920s, cracked and popped. Great-grandpa's eyes were glued to the action.

The film cracked and popped as scene after scene rolled on without end. A young man swung an axe at another man who broke line at a corn grinding mill. Then, he lined his five teenaged boys up to whip them with plow lines, baling wire, and thorn bush limbs until their backs, butts, and legs streamed blood, cursing and belittling them all the while. A middle-aged, well-mustached man marched out into the street of a small town named Reform to have a shootout with a man who looked to be his older brother. Great-grandpa drew his pistol, then took three shots at the man in front of him, just like in a Marshal Dillon gunfight. Only the man he wounded was himself.

The scenes changed quicker than I could keep up with.

Next, a graying older man wearing all black shot a black woman between the eyes, on her own porch, simply because she wouldn't stop cursing him.

The last scene was of an old toothless black man, the only person standing over Great-grandpa's grave. He repeated the same sentence over and over. "My daddy was the meanest man in the whole county."

The movie ended and immediately restarted. It just kept looping over and over. It never changed, never showed scenes of his childhood. That's what I'd been told all my life—what happened in childhood didn't matter, no matter how devastating, as long as I knew I was loved. That's when it came to me why Great-grandpa was stuck. He never acknowledged or dealt with how wrongly he was treated as a child. He didn't know how. All he had were memories of those events that resulted in anger, violence, and abuse from what he had suffered as a child. The damnable misery of it all was he didn't know that was why he was stuck.

It was a problem, a trait, that certainly had been passed down.

Great-grandpa leaned forward, becoming more intensely interested in the story the longer he watched. He just kept smiling as he vigorously chewed his tobacco. He'd spit and then sip from his moonshine jug. The more excited he became, the less he remembered I was standing in front of him. Eventually, he just looked right through me, eyes glazed over like a blind man's. He laughed and slapped his knee as the scenes rolled on. The longer he watched, the less he realized he was the star of this movie, poorly played by the lead actor.

It hit me. "So, that's it. He can't escape the life he's made for himself."

"*You have become aware.*" The Great Voice boomed with approval.

It was like seeing a blinding sunrise for the first time. I knew what I had always known but had never acknowledged it.

Great-grandpa so loved the reputation of being the meanest man in the county that sitting in his rocking chair with his tobacco, moonshine, and pistol became his eternity. He was stuck in a half-way house between two worlds, seen and unseen. He enjoyed it because he didn't have to do anything different.

Great-grandpa turned and growled, "What in the hell are you talking about?"

I didn't answer.

The Great Voice whispered, "*The past is simply a prison of your own making from which only you can choose to escape.*"

Great-grandpa was so absorbed in his past life, he couldn't hear the Great Voice in the present. His future ended in this place forever.

I wanted to help him. "It's you, Great-grandpa. Don't you see? The movie is about you."

"It is? Well, ain't that something? You know, I kind of enjoy it. I really don't want it to stop."

"Why not?"

"Because it's all I've got."

I knew then this was not for me to fix. It was not why I was here.

The Great Voice spoke in the tone of a college professor. *"Fixing your past is not your purpose. Fixing your future is."*

I had to leave Great-grandpa and the worst parts of my family history and upbringing to have a clear vision of what I needed to do to help Naomi.

The Great Voice declared, *"Refuse the truth you have spoken, and I will create a new screen showing the story of your life, except this one will have sound. It will become your eternity."*

I didn't want that at all.

Great-grandpa continued staring at the screen, reliving every scene as if it was yesterday, laughing, drinking, and spitting tobacco. He neither acknowledged the hurt and pain he had received as a child nor that which he had inflicted upon his family—the destruction that eventually traveled down through the generations to my father. And to me. He chuckled at his deeds and exploits, oblivious to the consequences for all who followed after him. The rolling caption at the bottom of the screen told all the things he'd refused to change that could have spared our family great harm and destruction.

"Can you read, Great-grandpa?"

"Never took the time. Always too much work to do on the farm. And I'm too old to learn now. I'm all right. You don't have to worry about me."

Those last words were too familiar. I'd said them many times.

I figured he didn't want to learn because he knew the words would reveal the truth of the only identity he had left. If he read them, he would have to do something with them. Change.

I dared to say, "If nothing else, you could at least admit what you've done."

He glared at me. "Enough of that. I don't want to talk about it anymore, you hear?" The fury of his anger was hot, like a blast of wind blowing across a burn pile after land clearing, full of cinders and glowing ash. He had become imprisoned in a life of his own making. He enjoyed his anger, hate, meanness, and violence.

There was nothing I could do about it or for him. Nothing I could do except do something about me.

There was only one credit at the end of the movie, a title. *The Life and Times of the Proudest and Meanest Man in the County.* The film immediately started again before Great-grandpa had time to think about it.

Off in the distance, that same dark, gravelly voice from the abyss chuckled again. "See, I told you. You can't escape what made you who you are."

The longer Great-grandpa watched and smiled, the more shriveled he became, until he was just skin and bones. But he never took his attention from the screen. When the movie of his life restarted, he returned to his youthful appearance, and the process started again, aging him with every new scene. He must've gone through this cycle a million times.

He spat again, then turned up his jug.

I walked away sad, clutching the agate against my chest. The light in the agate swirled so brightly that it blocked out the picture screen.

"Wait." Great-grandpa stood and stretched, blinking his red and bewildered eyes.

"Are you coming with me?"

"No child, I can't. At least, not now. No one has come to help me leave this place."

"I will. I don't want to leave you like this, but I don't know what to do."

"No, it is not for you to do. There is only one you may help."

"How can I do this?"

"How to do such a thing comes from what you already know."

"I don't know what you mean."

"Be who you are and remember why you were created. You know what that is." He immediately sat down in his rocking chair and fixed his attention on the movie again, grinning and firing his pistol at the picture show screen.

Something, or someone, sat me down hard on a wooden straight-back chair that Great-grandpa's son, my papaw, once made. Shameful memories of my own deeds of hate, anger, and violence flashed before me on a movie screen like Great-grandpa's. Things I had denied coming from my birth family. Things I'd done because of what had been done to me.

In the first scene, Dad whipped me for "being bad at church" until my legs bled and whelps covered my backside.

My mother stood by and watched with her hand over her mouth but did nothing to stop him.

In the next scene, I was sketching our family dog while sitting in my favorite reading chair as a kid, only to have the sketch pad slapped out of my hands.

Dad screamed, "You should be outside playing baseball like a real boy and not a sissy."

Next, I was a teenager being blamed for something I didn't do. My father front- and back-handed me seven times across the face. I took it so that my little brother, who was at fault, wouldn't receive the punishment. The same young man, though less recognizable a few weeks later, slashed his older brother with a hunting knife to end years of bullying. A twinge of satisfaction tickled my heart watching that scene, though I didn't know why.

After that, a young man who seemed vaguely familiar lifted another man who'd cursed him. In a fit of rage, he raised him above his head, then slammed him down on the pavement in front of a crowd of his peers.

"That was the right thing to do," I whispered.

In the following scene, the same young man shot up a country store at midnight simply because the owner refused to sell him a cold drink when he walked shirtless past the sign on the wall that read, "No shirt, no shoes, no service."

"Who was that guy?" I asked.

Then, a newly married man became violent with his bride but never understood why.

"That man? I don't know him at all." I turned to Great-grandpa, who was lost in his own story. "Who is that?"

He spat his tobacco and took a swig of moonshine. "Ha! That's the part of me you inherited. Can't you tell?"

It dawned on me that not only had I done wicked things because of what was done to me by the hands of others, but I also had done things by my own hands because of what had been done to me. That's because I had not become aware or refused to change. Either way, the damage was done.

I looked back at the screen and for a moment saw clearly. It was me with the face of a demon. The man I was never supposed to become.

Great-grandpa's face turned into a skull, laughing. "Aren't you proud of your heritage, great-grandson? I am."

The next movie scene was me holding my son up by the collar because he'd said something disrespectful. The same violence inflicted on me as a young man I inflicted on my son. I'd had enough and turned away from the screen.

Great-grandpa squeezed my arm. "See why I stay here? I could never leave this place. Where could I go? No one in my family wants me around."

That hurt beyond bearing.

Something pinched the hairs on the back of my neck, and I glanced back at the screen. There in the corner, the face of my son's mother grinned with the venomous fangs of no forgiveness and the fiery eyes of grudge-holding. SHE wielded a big hammer with the word revenge written on it. I shuddered at the power over me that I had wrongly surrendered to her. I closed my eyes, realizing what I had done. The power that made me fearless against bullies made me feared in my own home. I had perpetrated violence, and the threat of more, against the family I had promised to love and protect.

"I failed them miserably," I cried.

I looked back at Great-grandpa. He was staring at me with clear, deep blue eyes. He spat out his tobacco, grabbed his moonshine jug, then slung it at the screen of his life before him with the force of a mighty man. It exploded, then the screen disappeared.

"Enough!" He marched over to me. "What you are attempting now, I could never do. Before you can go farther, you must turn loose of the damage your birth family inflicted on you and its power over you. You must give up the notion that the strength you possess from anger, hate, and violence ever gave you a lick of power. Destroy the picture show screen of your past. Relinquish how much you enjoy watching yourself. Let no one, not even SHE, hold you back."

Who is SHE?

But I knew exactly who SHE was.

"Leave it all where it lives, in the past, but never forget what you left behind as you open yourself to what's ahead."

"It stops here." I picked up the hard, straight-back chair made of the sins of my fathers passed down to me, then smashed the screen of my life. It exploded into a million shards of flaming glass that scattered in a blast of wind.

Great-grandpa chuckled, "Sometimes it takes a little bit of violence to shatter a whole lot more. I'm proud of you. Would you sit for a while?" He returned to his rocking chair, passed down through our family for generations. Funny thing, it had a fresh, new coat of paint.

I sat at his feet and spoke with him for a long time about my false pride and our family's violent past. He told many stories of how his father and his before him handed down the anger, violence, and abuse from generations long past. His wisdom had broken through the barriers of his own wrongs he had enjoyed for decades.

"You must release the hold your birth family has on your soul to reach Naomi."

"You know about her?"

"I do."

"How?"

"I think I know who my great-great-granddaughter is. She passed by here not long ago and stopped to stare at me. She seemed a little uncomfortable. I figured you'd be close behind."

"This place isn't what I thought it'd be, Great-grandpa."

"Ain't it so?" He hung his head. "I'm sorry I couldn't defeat the anger that's been in our family for so long. I got it honest, as they say, and I did hand it down to your papaw, who passed it to your father, who in turn infected you. Forgive me, great-grandson."

"All is forgiven."

He whispered, "What has caused you much grief and heartache in life must be broken here. Otherwise, you will never find Naomi."

I took his hand. "It stops here."

Great-grandpa sat up straight and looked into the sky. "I give up all." He faded back into his seat, shut his eyes with a sigh, then fell asleep, snoring lightly. As I watched, he disappeared into a vapor of light.

"*The chains of generational sin have now forever been broken,*" The Great Voice trumpeted in the sound of a thousand voices.

I sat in the rocking chair of my fathers and reflected for a while on what had just happened and what had changed. My ancestors had been redeemed. I needed to find my redemption.

The Great Voice sighed with relief. "*Now the path in the swirls of the agate will guide you.*"

Granny appeared in a mist. "Now go, find your mercy seat."

I stood up, renewed. "I can go do this now."

When we find ourselves in some danger, we must not lose courage,
but confide much in the Lord; for where danger is great,

great also is the assistance of Him who is called
our Helper in tribulation.

—*St. Ambrose*

CHAPTER 45

The Second Descent

If the doors of perception were cleansed,
then everything would appear as it actually is, Infinite.

—*William Blake*

CAUTIOUSLY STEPPED back onto the descending path. What would come next?

"Doesn't matter. I'm going."

"*You have released the wounds done by the hands of others,*" the Great Voice thundered once again. "*Acknowledge now your greatest hurt.*"

"What is my greatest hurt?"

Silence. Again. Of course.

As I walked, I recounted all the horrible things I could think of that had damaged my thoughts and feelings. "Which was the worst hurt, the greatest pain? Could I even recall it? Have I blocked it so well I may never retrieve it from some dark corner in my mind? Was it that I could not measure up to standards that were never mine in the first place? Was it that I had become an out-of-control overachiever, trying to prove my worth to someone who couldn't care less about the true person I was? Where is this mercy seat, anyway?" I stopped talking. It was doing me no good.

I came upon a large rock shouldered on the back of one of my graduate school professors. He was the worst mentor I had ever experienced in my thirty-year career in ministry. He was singing, "I will work, I will pray, in the vineyard, in the vineyard of the Lord...."

Though claiming to pray for me often throughout my years in ministry, he created work expectations and achievements I couldn't live up to, nor should have ever had to. They weren't mine. But because my father had done that same thing to me growing up, I was trained well to surrender my identity to please another. I couldn't fight off my unhealthy need to be affirmed by a father figure. I bought into his poor mentoring hook, line, and sinker. I "drank the Kool-Aid" as they say, and my family was the worse for it. I don't blame him. I made my own choice. But he should've known better.

As I walked closer, I fell to all fours. My legs and arms became legs with hooves, and my body from the neck down became that of a large mule. It felt strange to swish a tail.

My mentor smiled, even in the pain and strain of bearing the weight of his own making.

A heavy leather harness dropped on my shoulders, and a large, two-wheeled cart was dragged up behind me by the same creepy demons at the bridge. They were chained together and wearing old-style prison suits with stripes. As they hitched me to the cart, I tried to run. The demons held me in place.

My mentor yelled, "Load the cart, boys. Don't worry about the mule. He's a strong one. If he can't pull the cart, we'll just get another mule. They're a dime a dozen anyway." He laughed as he lowered the load from his back to the ground.

Dressed in university graduation garb, my mentor grabbed my bridle to hold me in place. "You have graduated to shoulder the unreasonable burden of ministry. I'm so proud of you." He sang, "I want to be a worker for the Lord," and continued humming the tune as the demons loaded his burden onto my cart.

Large rocks that took two demons to lift into my cart had words written on them. My mentor stood by, pen and paper in hand, checking each off like taking inventory—preach more, study more, teach more, serve more, write more, work harder, late nights, eighty-hour week, sacrifice all, family comes second, no vacations, only I can do it, family will understand, do it for God, and on and on. As the pile grew higher in my cart, my mentor threw in a master's degree diploma and a plaque for good service, then a second master's degree and an article about my ministry published in a Christian magazine, then a doctorate diploma and a plaque for the grade point average award, then an adjunct professor position at his seminary, and finally recommendations to serve on prestigious boards. The cart's wheels sunk deeper into the ground with every accolade he offered.

The demons finished loading my mentor's burden of expectations. He seemed so pleased with himself. "All right, that's enough for now. We'll add more later."

Like an out-of-control mule, I brayed, "More, I can do more."

Where did that come from?

My mentor crossed his arms in pride. "Good, that's very good. I've trained you well." He kneeled to pray. "Lord, give my student strength to do all I expect him to do, even beyond his abilities, so I can boast about my good job training him." He rose and skipped away to look for another victim, singing, "He wants to be a worker for the Lord…."

"Where are you going?"

"Home to be with my family. My burden is lifted. It's yours now. I expect great things from you. Be warmed and filled."

I strained to pull the weight, but the cart wouldn't move. It was stuck. In a rut of my own making.

"How did I ever get myself into this? Never did I believe this was what Creator wanted for me in the first place."

Around my neck was a gold chain with all the awards and special recognitions I'd received. My family was nowhere to be found. I cried because I had imprisoned myself.

A small light crested on the hill to my right. There stood Naomi as a young child, waving. "When are you coming home, Daddy?"

I strained to break free of the harness that shackled me. I cried until there were no more tears. I screamed, "I sacrificed all to please someone else. I gave up the true me who never would have forgotten his family."

Naomi happily skipped over the hill, not understanding the damage I had done to her or myself.

But I did in that moment.

The Great Voice spoke, offering comfort. *"There It is. The "I" you must now regain."*

How foolish I must've looked all those years, running around like a chicken with its head cut off, trying to please men more foolish than I in how they served in ministry.

I looked down at my mule hooves and legs. "I'm nothing but a dumbass."

"Yes, my son, that you have surely been."

Consolation from the Great Voice should have soothed me, but it got my dander up. "Well, thank you very much."

"You are not welcome."

I stopped straining against the harness. "I've felt that way a long time but couldn't bring myself to think about it. It hurts too much."

"Why?"

"I don't want to say."

"Why?"

My anger burned within. "I could never do enough to please you."

"Did I ever tell you that?"

I didn't want to answer. "No." I needed someone to blame. Creator was convenient.

"Think about who did."

"My teachers, my mentors, my colleagues, my—"

"No. Not any of them."

I slumped, weak, as if I'd been pulling the cart uphill all day. "I'm so tired of this game."

"You've played it quite well, and for some time. Aren't you exhausted with yourself?"

"With myself? Didn't my mother always want me to be a 'good gospel preacher?' I thought Dad would finally be proud of me for doing what he thought was the greatest thing a man could do—become a minister."

"Nothing wrong with being a preacher, is there?"

"There is when you do it for the wrong reason."

"What wrong reason would that be, my son?"

"To please people who cared more for how I made them look than about who I was."

"And who was that?"

"My dad, who belittled the things I was created to do, and my mother who overplayed me being her favorite. I caught hell on every turn from my brothers and father because of her. My mentors who praised me for doing things beyond their abilities but took credit for my successes."

"So, they made the choice to become a minister for you?"

"Didn't they?"

"How could they?"

I could feel the presence of the Great Voice walking away. Had Creator given up on me?

"Have I ever?"

The Great Voice had read my thoughts. Then again, didn't He always?

"No. I'm still just a dumbass harnessed to a cart filled with someone else's burdens."

The Great Voice's fading words rang true in my ears. *"You said it. I didn't."*

I yelled out after Creator, "So, is this how you left Adam to fend for himself?"

The Presence of the Great Voice returned with such force, I was knocked down and the cart flipped over. *"He walked the path he chose for himself!"*

The heat of a thousand suns roasted my face, but my flesh did not melt. I mumbled getting back up, "Boy, did I ask the wrong question."

"*Yes, you did.*"

"I've just about had all of this I can stand. I don't know what to do next. I don't know where I need to go. I just want to be free of this load I'm expected to bear."

The Great Voice consoled me, His words soft like the trickle of water. "*I do understand.*"

"Creator, all I want to do is walk with you in the cool of the day like Adam did before it all went to hell."

"*You will if you continue.*"

"How can I, when I'm hitched to this overloaded cart?"

"*Once again, my son, you have answered your own question.*"

"You mean I did this to myself?"

No response.

"Yes, I did this to myself."

"Now you're talkin'," Great-grandpa's voice echoed.

The harness disappeared, and the cart rolled away. Never had such a heavy burden lifted from my soul as this.

Not all storms come to destroy your life; some come to clear the path.

—Unknown

CHAPTER 46

A Seeking Soul Set Free

"No" might make them angry but it will make you free. If no one has told you, your freedom is more important that their anger.

—Nayyirah Waheed

REE OF THE cart, I ran as fast as my four legs would take me. My pace slowed, but I was still worried I wouldn't escape. My body morphed back into its naked human form. I stopped and looked back. Nothing and no one chased me. Though relieved to be myself again, I still felt like the dumbass I'd been for so long. I kept walking. Fast.

My university professor and mentor screamed after me, "No one will ever honor you. You will never receive a standing ovation. Your name will never be written in a book anywhere. You won't be remembered by anyone for anything."

I'd heard that before.

I left him behind with all the accomplishments and laurels of perceived great ministry. None of that mattered in this place, nor anywhere else for that matter. Besides, there was only one book I wanted my name in anyway. But that wasn't my first goal. I had something much more important to do today.

I stopped to rest and reflect on what had just happened. I sat at the edge of a large clearing littered with tree stumps of every shape and size yet to be removed. The trees had been taken down with axes and burned, but the stumps remained steadfast in the soil. Undoubtedly, the workers did everything they knew to remove them but had given up.

A huge wall with ancient Egyptian carved reliefs emerged out of the ground in the center of the field, a great trumpet announcing its arrival. The once-famous people with no names eyed each other with blank stares. They were the elite whose names and exploits were to be remembered throughout the ages. At least, that's what they had been told. Their fancy headwear and expensive clothes revealed they had enjoyed the very best of what the human race had to offer. Men and women had kneeled before them, even worshipped them as gods..

"What are their names, and who remembers them now? Who even knows what these people did or accomplished?"

No one, absolutely no one.

My heart felt sad for all the men and women who spent so much energy trying to be rich and famous, ruling over people like they owned them. And when they got what they wanted, it was still not enough. They loved to be center stage. And the toll on other humans? Well, it was incalculable.

"What can I say?" I too loved the praise and wanted to be remembered as much as them for my service to the poor and homeless. I enjoyed being the expert "go to" guy about the culture of poverty, though never was I poor myself. I thought about the book and many articles I'd written with such confidence in my knowledge about the poor and working among them when no one else would. I had been up close and personal with the most reviled people on earth—drug dealers, prostitutes, traffickers. I even embraced them and was proud of myself for my accomplishment. I acted as though I didn't love the praise and attention, but the truth is, I savored it. Like the Egyptians in the carved reliefs, I wanted my name to be remembered throughout the ages.

Creator whispered, *"Confession is good for the soul, even if no one hears it but you."*

Rested, I was handed a pick and shovel. I went to work in the great field of stumps. With each uprooted stump, the need for recognition that destroyed my family became clearer. I had failed to make them, especially Naomi, most important in my life.

The great trumpet sounded, and the figures on the relief turned and stared at me with lifeless eyes. I just kept digging and straining to get the stumps out of the ground.

I wiped the sweat from my brow. "This is hard work." In just a short time, it was like I had been rooting up stumps all day but had hardly gotten anywhere. But with confessing each wrong, I felt better about myself than I had in years. I stopped again to rest and take stock of what I'd accomplished.

I looked out across the field of endless stumps. "I have a long, long way to go."

Another ancient stone relief of important, though nameless, Egyptians rose from the ground to block my path. The largest figure, wearing a huge crown, was surrounded by dignitaries and servants who bowed before him. The crowned figure had my face carved into its stone head. Another figure with a familiar face stood behind me with his hand on my shoulder—my mentor.

He never stopped repeating his mantra. "He's my student. The more he does, the more credit I receive. Praise him."

I was flummoxed, uncertain of my next steps. A hammer and a chisel dropped at my feet. Then, I knew what I had to do. My stone face changed from laughing to crying to anger to joy with every blink of the carved eyes as I neared the relief, hammer and chisel in hand. The figure was so tall and stately, something to be admired.

My face on the relief became my father's worst demeaning expression. He spoke words I'd heard since I was a child. "You will never amount to anything if you do that."

My face immediately returned on the carved relief.

I raised the chisel and swung the hammer with all my might. "I should've taken my licks and followed my own heart. I just wasn't strong enough as a child or as an adult."

The face on the carved relief that was mine broke off in one chunk and landed on the ground.

The face that was mine smiled and blinked its eyes. "You can still put me back up there. You're going to miss all the attention you so desperately seek."

I shook my head.

"You still have time." The kind, gentle voice became dark and gravelly, like that of the Great Serpent from the abyss. "You'll feel so much better about yourself if you do. You'll prove to your father and your mentor you are worthy."

I threw away the chisel and raised the hammer high. "I can do this." I slammed the hammer into the stone face with all my might, then stood back. My assault had no effect whatsoever except for a huge smile that broke out on the relief.

"I like it when you try to destroy your own image, the one you have carved for yourself for so long now. I'm so talented and so beautiful, don't you think?"

I raised the hammer to strike again, and the face that was mine screamed, "Do it again! The harder you try to break your own image, the stronger I become. I feed on your anger, lies, and self-hate. Please hit me harder. I'm hungry."

I didn't know what to do except cry out, "I can't do this."

Granny swept by in a flash as I stood in the midst of thousands of dead and rotting stumps. In a thunderclap, she announced as she pointed at me, "You'll wound his head." She glared at the relief face. "And you will wound his heel."

I jumped straight up, as high as I could, and smashed the carved face into a thousand pieces with my bare foot. But not before the stone face bit a chunk of flesh from my heel. The burning pain was excruciating as the venom invaded my leg.

Laughter erupted, and the gravelly voice from the abyss sang Granny's words in an old familiar tune as I rubbed my bleeding foot. "It shall bruise thy head, and thou shalt bruise his heel." I'd always known Satan sung the same songs I did growing up in church.

I asked the Great Serpent, "And how's that been working for you?"

The Great Serpent sneaked toward me from behind the stumps, never breaking eye contact. It rose to face me like a king cobra.

Peering into the eyes of the great snake that could swallow me whole made me shudder.

"Very well, thank you very much. The wound on your heel will never heal. My venom is strong. You will limp wherever you go, my friend."

"I'll be fine."

"I can make it better if you like," the Great Serpent hissed.

Every accolade and recognition I'd ever received, but had just left behind, buzzed all around me like large horseflies fighting each other to land and take a bite. I swatted at them to keep from being bitten, but they became thick as a cloud. I couldn't think about anything but the attacking insects. They swooped in, snatching bloody bites, then flew away, until they all landed on me at once. Their job was done. They had blocked my every effort to look within my soul while I fought them.

I didn't know what to do, but I knew what I wanted to do. I wanted to be relieved of proving myself to anyone and discard all my awards. The only thing I could think of was to squeeze the agate still in my hand. Immediately, a rainbow beamed across the field, its shine so bright it chased the horseflies of my achievements and awards away.

The sly serpent chuckled. "You will never forget your need for self-importance. The wound of your own bite never heals. It only festers."

"My bite?"

"Yes, the one you took when just a child."

"I don't remember that."

"Remember when you wanted a baseball trophy so badly? You cried so hard when you didn't get it."

I pictured my dad screaming at me playing baseball poorly when I was only nine years old. I decided then that I would do whatever it took to please my father. It cost me my soul.

"That bite, my friend, will be with you always. It's my gift to you from the Garden."

"Yes, it will be with me forever. But now I know it. Your mistake again, Great Serpent. You've brought to the light what was long hidden in the shadows. Don't you know awareness is the beginning to conquer any problem? It may never completely go away, but I see it for exactly what it is, and I see you for exactly who you are. Every time the bite stings, I'll be reminded of your wicked schemes."

The Great Serpent remained still as the figures in the stone relief, except for moving his head side to side, searching my eyes for weakness and trying to charm my soul. He inched forward, coaxing me to surrender.

The longer I held out against the intensity of his gaze, the weaker I became. My spiritual energy drained like a body bleeding out. Dreamy visions of The Palace of Ten Thousand Delights flickered through my brain.

I was startled back to my senses by the moist heat and foul stench of the Great Serpent's fetid breath. His head was mere inches from mine, and his gaping maw revealed fangs, stained and covered with rotting flesh. He reared back, prepared to strike and inject his deadly venom into my heart before succumbing to his insatiable appetite and swallowing me whole.

Despite the danger, I didn't care that he was ready to engulf me. I felt no pain. Felt nothing but relaxation and pleasure. He was too strong for me to overpower or overcome. I couldn't break the trance. My only exit was the red staircase leading to the bright lights of the palace, and that was no escape. Resigned to my fate, I held up my arms to receive what I deserved.

A slight breeze passed by, reminiscent of the one I felt when searching for the Name Tree. A familiar face wearing the familiar flowing gown of a swirling multicolored agate spoke in the familiar tone of the same trickling small stream that flowed beside the tree where I carved Naomi's name.

"I know that face." My tone was weak and slow with weariness.

"You can do this," Granny said.

With my last bit of strength, I slapped the agate against my forehead. Naomi's smiling face popped in my head. Blue flames danced around me, and I was filled with the strength of a great warrior.

My adversary reeled back, surprised.

"I know who you are, and you will not have me!"

The Great Serpent cried a monstrous hiss. He slithered into a hole where a large stump had been removed. As its tail disappeared, his laughter grew. "We shall see. Oh, yes, we shall see."

Granny consoled me with a question. "What is a true purpose if untested?"

I sat on the ground to rest.

Lean into the experiences you avoid.

—Unknown

No one escapes the wilderness on the way to the Promised Land.

—Annie Dillard

CHAPTER 47

Dad

Criticism, like rain, should be gentle enough to
nourish a man's growth without destroying his roots.

—*Frank A. Clark*

FTER THE FOUL-smelling serpent disappeared, every remaining stump began sinking into the ground behind him. My strength returned as I clutched the agate. The stumps of my awards and achievements completely disappeared. My stomach was in knots, like when Dad was disappointed with me for bringing home a C on my report card instead of an A. I sat still until the feeling left me.

I crossed the great barren field now empty of stumps. In the far corner, someone—blurry to me at that distance—vigorously worked in a small garden. As I approached, he didn't look my way and continuously wiped the sweat pouring from his head, drenching his shoulders and the back of his blue overalls.

Disgust souring his features, he threw down a stained handkerchief and mumbled, "Why can't I get anything to grow in this garden? The soil's rich, and the seeds are good. We've had the right amount of sunshine and rain. These boys just won't grow. I must not be holding my mouth right."

"Dad, is that you?"

He didn't acknowledge me for a moment, being too focused on his failing work. He glared right through me as if I wasn't there. "I didn't expect to find you here."

My two brothers' heads and mine continuously burst from the ground like new sprouts. In his effort to keep invisible weeds at bay, he cut us down before we could sprout up out of the soil. The dirt would crack open, then we would reach for the limitless sky. But the sharp blade of abusive religion and our violent family history Dad never dealt with ended our promising dreams before they could begin to be realized. Many were severed. The few withstanding his efforts still withered and died.

Dad looked to Heaven for help. "Why won't this work? I can't figure it out. I'm doing everything right. It must be their fault they can't grow. Bad seed. It must be bad seed." He just chopped harder and faster, frustrated, the sweat pouring from his face.

Yeah, whose seed?

Weeds popped up all around my brothers and me. As we tried to sprout, all the things Dad did to hurt us sprung up to choke the life out of us. He no longer chopped us down. He went after the weeds using his hands with all of his might.

Mom stood at the screen door of the house I grew up in. She held a plate of freshly baked cookies and watched in tears but never said a word to Dad about his behavior.

Just young children we were, but for all we did to break through the encrusted earth and choking weeds, we simply became bruised reeds never given the chance to bloom.

How did we even survive at all?

The Great Voice whispered, "*You forget I held back the blade of Abraham to save Isaac. Someone once allowed terrible things to be done to His Son, or have you forgotten so quickly?*"

"But why did you let it go on so long?"

"I do not allow bruised reeds to break."

"But so much was broken back then. Some things beyond repair."

"Not so much that you could not be here, I think."

"But why me?"

"Someone had to break the chain of generational anger, violence, and abuse."

"But why me?"

"And why not you?"

"I have nothing, not even my clothes."

"Do you really need them?"

"I guess not. Just another prop to keep me from seeing the true me, I guess. I'm still not sure why You chose me."

"You have ventured beyond into the place most fear to dare."

"I don't understand."

"Yes, you do. And soon you will become aware."

"How do you know that?"

"You really want to ask me that question?"

"Yes, I do."

The harder Dad pulled at the weeds, the angrier and more violent he became. The quicker the weeds returned, the easier it was for him to blame us boys for not becoming what he wanted us to be—little men created in his image, not Creator's.

"Why don't they look like, walk like, talk like, act like… me, me, me?" he chanted as he thrashed the weeds with his bloody and calloused hands in rhythm with his words, a mournful dirge in answer to my pain.

Dad never learned the true Hebrew meaning of the proverb that parents should train a child in his own way rather than expecting him to become a little clone with no thought given to who Creator made the child to be.

Frustrated, Dad threw up his hands and walked over to a lone shade tree.

I followed him.

"Why won't they just do right?" After taking a long drink from the same blue and white Igloo water jug we had when I was a kid, he sat, crossed his legs, then began sharpening a hunting knife he'd made for me years ago. He rubbed the blade in a consistent circular motion on a gray whetstone. About every ten revolutions, he would thumb the blade to test its sharpness. It was the same knife I had cut my older brother with when I'd finally gotten fed up with his incessant bullying. I was only seventeen then.

"Dad."

Without looking up or stopping his sharpening, he spoke in a subdued, almost defeated voice I'd never heard before. "I've been waiting. I wasn't sure you'd want to come see me, son." He stopped sharpening the knife and looked me in the eye. "Do you want me here?"

"I've always wanted you with me, Dad."

"I'm glad." His hazel eyes sparkled in the summer sun, and his eyebrows arched in pleasant recognition. He grinned as he restarted his sharpening. His sweaty overalls and shirt were covered with arrowheads I'd found, toy soldiers I once played with, poems and short stories I'd written, drawings I'd sketched, and many other things important to me, things he once belittled me for as a child. Also on them were pages from the Bible he had given me on my eighth birthday. All these things crawled around on his clothes like carpenter bees trying to burrow into a hard oak post. They weren't succeeding.

His bare feet were covered with the sand of the many creeks and rivers I'd wandered. He donned a baseball cap from the team I'd quit at ten years old because he said I was the worst player he'd ever seen. He told me one night, after I'd failed miserably in a game we'd lost, that I played worse than a girl. I never played organized baseball again, nor let him come to any of my other sporting events after that.

I peeked over his shoulder to see the three diplomas of my two master's degrees and doctorate attached to the back of his shirt. A couple years before I went back to college at age twenty-eight, he told my friends if I went back to school for ministry, I'd fail because I didn't know how to study. I remembered receiving the award for best doctoral dissertation and a perfect 4.0 grade point average. I wanted to share that honor with him and the other awards and achievements I'd garnered, so he would love and accept me.

When the graduation ceremony ended that day, he barked, "Give me your keys, I need to go pack." He left the auditorium, went to my apartment, packed, then went home, but he never congratulated me. Then, like so many other times, I just wanted him to be proud of me. To approve of me. That desire never went away, not even as an adult.

It never once happened. He never gave me, or my brothers, his blessing.

Off in the distance, from the dark shadows of a thick forest, came a familiar gravelly snicker. "Did I not tell you you'd never forget?"

The Great Voice bellowed out from the sky, strong and sudden as a summer cloudburst. *"Please only the one who matters most."*

I had to think about that for a moment. *Why do I have to be the best to please anyone?*

"How are you doing, Dad, being here?"

Dad stopped sharpening and shaved the hairs on his arm. Each one carried a hateful word he'd spoken, a violent outburst he had inflicted on me, or a missed opportunity to bless me and my brothers. They fell from his arm only to become red fire ants that crawled back up to their assigned places. After biting his arms, they became hairs again. He tried to brush them off, but they became embedded. He went back to sharpening the knife, gritting his teeth in the pain.

"I've been doing this for a long time, son. I can't seem to get them to leave. Their bites hurt, but I don't know what to do. I know it's not the ants, but I can't figure out what it is."

I wanted to take his pain away, but I'd tried and failed so many times before. "Why am I here with you, Dad?"

"You said you wanted me here."

I wasn't sure how this would go. Memories of my childhood flooded my mind like a huge dam had just broken and the water raged out of control. Dad beating me until I was bruised and bleeding, telling me I would never amount to anything, convincing me I was a sissy for quitting sports, and insisting I was stupid for being a history-loving writer and artist. Overwhelmed, I turned to walk away.

"We must all acknowledge truth in this place." He kept sharpening the knife.

"What do you need to acknowledge, Dad?"

In anger, he threw the knife and whetstone down like I'd seen him do so many times when he wasn't happy with something I had done. "That I did not believe in you. I refused to recognize God's gifts and potential in you. I was selfish and jealous of your talents. I gave it my best effort to stifle them because I had none myself."

"Who said you had no gifts or potential, Dad?"

"You know." I vaguely remember Dad telling us how his father had whipped him with plow lines, thorny briar limbs, and hay-baling wire for little or no reason. He'd only once mentioned how his mother belittled him and made fun of him because his dad favored him over all the other children. What a three-ring circus to be caught in the middle of, especially as the main attraction. I knew it well. My parents' roles were the reverse of his, but we both experienced the same abuses. How confusing that must've been to him. It was for me. But how could he not have seen himself repeating that behavior and visiting those cruelties on us?

Blood began trickling down his legs, running to his feet, then between his toes. "Your papaw raised us children like he trained our farm animals—beat and break them into submission so they could be obedient and useful. Your mamaw stood by and watched, belittling me every chance she got because I was his favorite."

He couldn't break the cycle. He wasn't chosen to.

"Dad, I'm sorry."

He teared. "Your papaw never understood a heavy hand breeds rebellion. Your mamaw couldn't grasp the depth or hurt words can inflict. My daddy told me I would never amount to anything in this world because I wasn't good enough. And my mother laughed and picked at me in my worst moments." He paused. In that brief moment, his chin came up, and his chest swelled. "But I'm proud to say that I never said anything bad about my daddy."

"Maybe you should have said something, Dad. To him and her, I mean."

"You didn't."

"I tried, but when you slapped me seven times across the face for standing up to you, I knew then it was a waste to keep trying. So, I left."

"I know, and I was wrong. I just didn't understand then what I know now. A man learns a lot about himself when he walks through the thin veil, travels from the seen into the unseen. Will you forgive me, son?"

I clutched the agate with the same strength as I had clung to my bad childhood memories about Dad. The harder I squeezed, the faster rivulets of dark and stinking bad blood sprouted like fountains from my pores. My compassion soared, as did my energy, with his confession and my forgiveness. How could I not feel for him? His father and mother had plagued him with the very same belittling words he pummeled me with all the years I was growing up.

"I have, Dad, but I do have a painful reminder of that night years ago."

"The jaw I slapped still hurts from time to time, doesn't it?"

"Yes."

"Believe it or not, in this place, every time you feel the pain in your jaw, Creator punishes me with the same, only ten times worse."

"I want the pain of that night to leave us both forever."

"I don't know how to do that. Do you, son?"

"Not yet, but I'm learning."

Dad went back to sharpening the knife.

"Why do you keep doing that?"

"I'm trying to make things better."

"Do you want them to be better?"

He stopped sharpening and sobbed for a moment. "Yes. Yes, I do."

"Why did you believe Papaw when he said you had nothing to offer the world?"

"I trusted my daddy's wisdom, though it was no wisdom at all. I expected you to trust me, even if it meant inflicting whatever punishment or abuse I thought necessary to make you be like me. I believed I was right about everything, just like my daddy."

I tried to lighten the mood a bit. "Yeah, I remember your favorite saying when I was in high school. 'It's my way or the highway.' It didn't work."

He didn't laugh. "I was too hard on you boys, like your papaw was with me, and I knew it. You boys became wild and sometimes out of control because of the way I treated you."

"Why did you always brag you had never said a bad word about your father?"

"I didn't want you to say a bad word about me."

"What was the worst part of it all?"

"You and your brothers becoming only half of what you should've been. I expected you to be like me and gave you hell about it if you weren't. I never blessed you for who Creator made you to be. I never learned the meaning of the words, 'Train up a child in his own way and he will never leave it.' I failed you, son."

I knew that was it. Thing was, I had learned it, too. But too late for Naomi.

I reached for his arm, but he pulled back from me. He wasn't done yet.

"Son, my anger was of the worst kind. Anger, really rage, at myself. I couldn't get past what my father had done to me enough to keep from doing the same things to you." He stopped sharpening and thumbed the knife edge. "That's about good enough."

"It's okay, Dad."

"No, it's not." He wouldn't look me in the eye. "I was wrong, son. That's all there is to it."

"Please put down the knife and whetstone."

He laid them down and looked at me.

I moved ever so slowly to sit on my dad's lap. My form shifted to that of a young child. I put my arms around his shoulders and kissed him on the neck. We sat still and quiet for a long time.

Dad sniffled. "That's the damnable misery of it all. I so appreciated what you were doing but was too mean, proud, and jealous to value your gifts. I am sorry, son."

"It's all right."

All the arrowheads, toy soldiers, poems and short stories, sketches, and pages from the small Bible—everything that I had held dear as a child—faded into his clothes. I felt a surge of energy flowing into his body and left his lap. He stood and shone like a ray of sunshine breaking through a thick summer storm cloud.

"Now I know who you are, son, and I am well-pleased. You have been wonderfully made in the image of Creator for His purpose. Be that. It is enough."

I returned to my adult self and stood proud. The warmth of his blessing wrapped around my entire body like a thousand electric blankets on a cold winter's night. "I believe I can go forward now."

Dad looked out at the great field and laughed. "Ain't it amazing how those stumps are gone?" He covered his forehead with his hand to shield his eyes. "My goodness, would you look at the size of those turnips? And that crookneck squash, it's as yellow as the sun. That okra is head-high, and the green beans weigh the bushes down to the ground. I better get to work." He started for the garden patch he'd been hoeing but turned and sat back down.

He dusted the sand from his bare feet and picked up his old, worn, leather work boots. He started to put them on but stopped, then handed them to me. "Take them. You'll need these where you're going next. Don't be afraid, son. I believe in you."

The strength of a thousand Samsons flowed into my soul.

Dad hugged me before disappearing into the beautiful field of all good garden things.

*The more anger towards the past you carry in your heart,
the less capable you are of loving in the present.*

—*Barbara De Angelis*

CHAPTER 48
The Third Descent

You cannot find yourself by going into the past.
You find yourself by coming into the present.

—Eckhart Tolle

I TROTTED DOWN the path, carrying Dad's work boots, following sounds of large, heavy equipment moving earth around. I wasn't sure which way to go until a raggedy old lime green Euclid dump truck passed by me. Strange, it looked exactly like one I once drove when I worked construction in Alaska as a young man. Those "old dogs," as my boss used to call them, had been used to build the Al-Can Highway during World War II.

I struggled down the rocky rutted road on my bare feet to a construction site where I once worked. My old boss stood tapping his foot on the frozen ground, checking at his watch. I hadn't seen him in years.

"Morning, Boss."

"What the hell is good about it, and where in the hell have you been?" That was the typical happy greeting I received so many times from a man I respected much and knew meant no harm.

"Well, I'm here now."

"Don't you know it's twenty-five below out here? We've been here all day waiting on you." A row of dump trucks was lined up to be loaded, diesel motors rumbling and smoking.

"I didn't know."

"Well, you do now. Quit screwing around and get your ass up in that front-end loader. We've got a mountain of material to move."

"Yes, sir." I sat on the frozen ground to put on Dad's work boots. After standing, I stomped around for a minute. "Perfect fit."

I was ready to take on the world.

One after another, empty trucks pulled up to be loaded. I scampered up the ladder and into the cab of the front-end loader I had once operated for weeks at a time. But when I looked at the controls, my mind went blank. It was as if it was the first time I'd ever tried to operate this machine. For the life of me, I couldn't remember how to run this huge piece of equipment.

I looked around for a manual or a schematic on the wall inside the cab. Nothing. Pressure mounted. The trucks kept lining up. I was behind before I even got started.

My boss threw his arms up in the air. "What's wrong now, you dork?" He climbed the ladder and entered the cab. "Move over. Have I not shown you how to operate this thing?"

I shook my head. "You never took the time, Boss. You were always too busy. I tried to learn it by myself just now but couldn't."

He winked and smiled. "Sorry, you are not a dork. I am for expecting you to know how to do something I never taught you. You can do this." He explained how to operate the equipment, then I gently moved the levers to practice. My old boss loved teaching a new construction hand how to do the work he loved so much, building new roads where there weren't any.

He pointed at the controls. "Now, you've got a special road that needs building. Only you can do it." He moved over to sit in the doorway of the cab. "Try it by yourself now. Move some material around, pick it up, and dump it. Get the feel for the machine before you load the first truck. Once you start, you can't stop or you will fail. And I won't have you failing."

"Thanks, Boss."

He stayed with me until I could do it myself. "That was just practice. Move in the rhythm of the machine, and the trucks will follow your command." He hopped off the loader, then stood back out of the way, rubbing his chin.

I moved forward to dig a full bucket of green, slimy material that reminded me of the gelatinous substance that oozes from a dead body.

The first driver pulled up to get loaded. It was the legalistic preacher we had at our church when I was growing up. He glared at me and moaned, "You don't deserve the grace of God for all you've done wrong. There aren't enough trucks to haul away your sin."

I didn't listen to him as I loaded the detestable smelling goo into the dump bed. He drove away in a truck. The company sign on the side read, "Never Good Enough to Make It into Heaven."

The next load was a dark gray substance like hardened clay that hit the dump bed hard. The sign on the door said, "Things I Refused to Give Back That Were Never Mine in the First Place." The ministry mentor who had loaded my cart earlier drove away laughing and saying, "You never could keep up with me, could you?"

The next truck door's sign offered a reminder of toxic relationships from my past. "Pleasing Men Who Care Nothing About Who You Are." An elder of the church where I had served shook his head in disappointment and shouted, "All we wanted was the most baptisms for the dollar. We didn't care how you got them or what you had to sacrifice to get them. We wanted to boast about the numbers."

As he drove away disgusted, I remembered the long hours I worked to help people be saved. Then, Naomi's face flashed before my eyes.

The Great Voice whispered, *"He could save others but not himself. Or his daughter."*

I didn't take time to help save Naomi because I was too busy trying to save others.

I screamed over the sound of the front-end loader, "I shouldn't have done that!"

The next load I dug was full of beautiful but broken and smashed marble stones. The board chairman of the ministry I started among the poor revved the truck engine. On the door were the words, "Ministry Empire Builders." He scowled and complained, "You never were up to the challenge. Your ministry was nothing but shambles."

The last truck rolled up on its own, like a remote-control toy. I emptied the last of the rotting mass of stinking muck into the dump bed of a truck that had no sign on the door.

"Where's the driver?"

My boss climbed up the ladder of the loader and motioned for me to get out. "That's the last of the trucks. You did a great job. I'm proud of you."

"But who drives that one?"

"You must decide." I climbed down from the loader as my boss drove away whistling an old tune that Buddy Holly wrote, entitled, "That'll be the Day."

Yelling erupted down the hill where all the trucks had lined up. The drivers were waiting on me. Some raised their fists in anger, while others shook their heads in disgust. Though there was no sign on the last door for me to read, I knew what had to be painted on its side.

I reached into the dump bed, grabbed a handful of gooey muck, then wrote one word. "Fear." But apparently that wasn't enough.

All the other trucks could not be emptied until I dumped this one into the bottomless abyss. I had to give fear back to the one who brought it from Hell below.

I was ashamed. I had allowed fear to make me work long hours in overwhelmingly stressful situations to prove to unspiritual men I could do more for God than they could ever imagine. I neglected my family to carve out my place of prominence in a ministry world where men were recognized for how many people came to their church and how many were saved by their hand. The same men lived by a ridiculous rule.

Load the wagon and don't worry about the mule. If the mule gives out, we'll just get another.

I remembered the day I fell for that line, and my two children's faces immediately popped into my mind. I traded being a father to them for notoriety, believing I was the savior of the poor.

I cried.

I admitted my inadequacy. I had allowed men skilled at imprisoning souls with the power of their religious position to lead me along with the unwary multitude into a false belief that by human goodness and accomplishment, I would be saved—essentially, do more to get more in the Kingdom of God. I was too broken inside to live up to the expectations of men whose hollow souls had plenty of grace, mercy, and peace, but only for themselves.

I was angry and hurt at the same time. My mother's expectations of me being her perfect little golden boy whom she wanted to grow up to become a great preacher had dominated my identity. I had bought into the fiction that doing something great would make my father proud. I had swallowed their expectations that I would never be able to measure up, ever, and believed them hook, line, and sinker.

Those beliefs had ruled my life for years. And they destroyed my family.

I screamed, "Why did I do that?"

The Great Voice cracked like lightning. "Their expectations were never yours."

I sat on a rock, weary and perplexed, looking at the boots Dad had given me. I thought about the signs on the trucks and what my boss said when I finished loading them.

I needed understanding and held up the agate. It blinked brightly for just a moment.

I looked down at the work boots again. At some point, each had been inscribed. One read, "Doting Mom," and the other, "Abusive Dad."

I knew what other two words should be painted on this dump truck. I untied the laces, pulled off the boots, then walked barefoot to the truck. A small, blue paint can waited for me, a paintbrush on top.

On the door, after the word "Fear," I added, "of Failure."

The engine revved, reverberating like a lion's roar upon catching its prey.

My task became clear. I hopped up into the cab, then grabbed the stick shift. "I have to lead this truck caravan down the hill to dump all the false teachings I have absorbed that will hold me back from finding Naomi."

And so, I did. Each truck disappeared as its load was dumped into the abyss until finally, mine was the only one left. I set the choke, put it in gear, set it rolling, then jumped out. The truck plummeted into a fathomlessly deep ravine, taking with it my fear of failure.

I had set myself free.

My boss rolled up in the front-end loader. "Good work. Now, finish the job."

"What else do I need to do?"

He pointed to a raging watery mud slide that filled the abyss like a river bed. "Get across that."

"How?"

"Weren't you paying attention?"

"I thought so."

"Take this loader, then do what with it?"

I studied the situation. The thick mud oozed through the bed of the creek like a lava flow. To my right sat a mound of the finest road building material I'd ever seen. All the things I could've done to build my life better through the years.

My boss climbed down the ladder on the side of the front-end loader. "Good, you know what to do. When you dump the last bucket of that solid rock material, don't stop. Keep going. It will be the foundation on which you cross. Otherwise, the mud flow will take you downstream with it. And trust me, you do not want to go where it's headed."

I scrambled up the ladder and into the loader. I worked as fast as I could, building my makeshift bridge, trying to stay ahead of the mud flow that was taking away part of what I had dumped each time. I'd worked my way close to the other side when a great wall of mud hurled my way. I had time for only one more load before the watery wall of destruction smashed my work. I wasn't sure I could make it across in time. The gap between my makeshift bridge and the other bank was still too wide.

I scooped up the last load and headed full speed to the end of my bridge, raising the bucket to dump.

When my wheels were ten feet from the last bit of my bridge, the shadow of mud tsunami blocked the sunlight. Its roar was deafening.

I dumped my load, then pushed the accelerator to the floor. The loader ramped off the ground, then landed in the gap between the end of my bridge and the bank on the other side. It was stuck and could go no farther. I scrambled out of the cab like a monkey, scampered across the front of my machine, then climbed onto the bucket.

The great wall of mud flow crashed against my makeshift bridge. As it collapsed, I dove to the other side.

When I landed, I looked back to find the loader had been swept away.

I lay on the ground, exhausted, watching the enormous swell of mud roll down the river bed, the loader tumbling end over end in the flow. In it were all the things the dump trucks had emptied. The mass disappeared into the darkness of the abyss that once had held my soul hostage.

I had given my sin back to the one bent on my destruction.

The dark, gravelly voice said, "And you think I'm done with you?"

I put the Great Serpent out of my mind. Across the creek, on the bank I'd just left, stood my boss and my dad, smiling and shaking hands.

I made it across, exhausted but happy for the first time since I'd been there. Dad yelled, "I always knew you could do it, son!"

I waved before turning to walk a newly cleared path. I didn't look back. I'd done that too many times and for long over the years. True life lay ahead in this place of death, and I was determined to find it.

When I found a bed of soft, green grass, I stretched out on the ground, then fell into restful sleep.

You can't go back and change the beginning
but you can start where you are and change the ending.

—*C.S. Lewis*

CHAPTER 49

Bittersweet is the Victory

*If we have no peace, it is because we have
forgotten that we belong to each other.*

—*St. Teresa of Calcutta*

I DREAMED I was sitting in my recliner in our home years ago. Seven-year-old Naomi timidly peered around the corner. She wanted something but wouldn't speak. Cautiously, she approached, rubbing her hands together, trying to decide if she would ask the question on her mind. She didn't have to.

I playfully grabbed her, tickled and cuddled her.

She giggled and squirmed until she fell fast asleep cradled in my arms.

I don't remember anything after that.

I didn't need to.

It was enough.

We fell asleep.

Peace.

Suffering invites us to place our hurts in larger hands.

—*Henri Nouwen*

CHAPTER 50
At Rock Bottom in the Abyss

Each of us is more than the worst thing we've ever done.

—*Bryan Stevenson*

GREAT ILLUMINATION SPARKLING bright as the light of exploding stars permeated my closed eyelids. Even then, I shielded my face. The glare was too much. Then, they disappeared, overshadowed by the smoke of a smoldering, smothering fire slowly consuming everything in sight.

My eyes opened to a calm, blue sky, swelling like an incoming tide that pushed aside the once raging fire. It revealed an eerie house like the one up the hill from where I grew up. We were always afraid to pass it on our way to catch the school bus. I'd once seen a ghost there, beckoning me into the destroyed home like a mother greeting her children after school. As I'd watched, her face turned from sweet to hideous, and I shuddered as I hurried past.

Nothing made sense in this place. Things changed too quickly. I took a deep breath and waited for it to come. Whatever it was.

For a split second, the burned down dwelling became a lavish house with many colorful stained glass windows and flower boxes full of every beautiful bloom imaginable. A sign above the entrance read, "The Golden Mansion of Happy Chaos." Then, the house melted. It became a dilapidated old warehouse like a building that had barely survived the nuclear bomb explosion at Hiroshima.

Faces appeared in the windows, hundreds of them, all wildly talking with every conceivable emotional human response possible, all at the same time. I couldn't understand anything they said. It was too much, too fast. I squinted through the dissipating smoke. The faces were all mine, each wearing a different colored t-shirt with a different emotion embroidered on the front.

"What's happening to me?"

The Great Voice said, *"You have asked the right question."*

An old monk in a brown habit quietly left the noisy house. I turned to follow him through a beautiful flower garden.

I knew this man, but he walked right past me. Though I never became a Catholic, he had once chatted with me at a mountain monastery, where I used to spend time alone to commune with Creator. His comfort and advice were exactly what I needed at the time. I poured out my soul. He listened to me. The solitude, stillness, and silence I had enjoyed in the seclusion of that monastery soothed and restored my soul more than once. But here he was, in this place, and I was comforted.

The old monk sat on a large, perfectly round gray rock the same color of his neatly trimmed beard. Actually, he wasn't sitting. He was hovering in the lotus position several inches above the perfect stone sphere with his eyes closed.

The confused and arguing faces in the windows of The Golden Mansion of Happy Chaos behind me grew so deafeningly loud, I couldn't think. I turned to silence them, but they captured my attention and started to take me hostage with their relentless chatter.

The monk growled, "Silence!"

The faces sulked. I jerked around at the power of his command.

The old monk still levitated above the perfectly round gray rock. Now, his eyes were blue flame, and his tongue a lash of red fire. "Let's invite the Spirit to join us."

Instantly, my entire body swelled like a toad to appear larger than lurking predators. Unimaginable strength like I'd never felt before surged through me. It was clearly not mine. It was being given to me. Strange, the rush didn't come from without, but from within. I shook myself and tried to steady my nerves.

The old monk faded into the perfectly round gray rock, but his message lingered. "Your soul has done well to become aware of that which your mind alone wants to command. For too long, selfish and out-of-control emotions have ruled your weak intellect, and in turn steered your soul wrongly."

For a moment, I wanted to be offended, but the power within spoke in unintelligible words I understood clearly.

The old monk continued. "The power within is now power sufficient if you let it be so."

My knees wobbled from the exhaustion of receiving this great power I did not understand.

He spoke again. "The power is not in the understanding but in the receiving. Who can understand the Great Within?"

I hugged the large, perfectly round gray rock, for it was the only thing tangible I could grab if I fainted and fell. "Are emotions wrong?"

"How could they be?"

"Somehow I know that, but I'm confused."

The old monk chuckled. "Now that is a great admission."

I waited for more knowledge.

"You need no more knowledge. You need only to practice that which you have already learned. Seek your own answer, but I will offer you this. Emotions are no more wrong than thoughts, as Creator made them both."

"Then how can any emotions be wrong if Creator made them and they are mine?"

"Only when you seek them and not when they seek you."

"As misguided thoughts can rule the mind, feelings can undo the heart. Is that it?"

The old monk emerged, then slid down the side of the perfectly round gray boulder. "Together they can imprison the soul if you let them."

I thought about that for moment. "Capture every thought and cast every care. Give them to the One who sits on the throne, makes things whole again, and holds the key."

The old monk faded away, and a small part of me went with him. "I will always have you in my heart, my son."

The Great Voice spoke, his tone encouraging. "*Seek balance. Naomi will not withstand your imbalance.*"

All the faces that were mine in the windows of the damaged old haunted-looking warehouse started up again, protesting with great riot. When I turned, The Golden Mansion of Happy Chaos glowed like a red sun, inviting me inside.

I calmed my soul and tried to capture every wayward emotion and useless thought. Slowly, the perfectly round gray rock opened a great mouth ready to swallow the chaos of my own making.

"I thought I had left it all behind on the other side of the putrid and muddy river."

The Great Voice spoke disparagingly. "*Are you still so dull? Only the tangibles and memories have been left behind. You still have far to go.*"

Emotions that had overwhelmed and overtaken me for so long and allowed me to enjoy sinful behaviors chaotically flooded my soul. The thousand faces that were mine pressed against the window panes of The Golden Mansion of Happy Chaos and screamed like the flesh was being ripped from their bodies, piece by piece.

My flesh.

My pain increased as demons appeared from nowhere to pelt me with every thought and emotion, digging their claws in deeper, trying to find a way into my soul.

"Leave!" I dropped to my knees in exhaustion as the demons stirred around me vigorously. I silenced my thoughts and calmed my heart.

A foundation emerged from the perfectly round gray rock, and a wall was slowly being constructed by unseen hands.

The demons didn't notice.

"Remove yourselves." I shuddered at their violent attempts to enter my soul.

Great blocks dropped into place at head height between me and the scratching and screaming demons. In a moment, I could barely see over the wall where the demons thrashed about like an out-of-control mob. Never had I heard such threats, cursing, and condemnation. Except every one of the thousand voices was mine.

The most hideous of the demon horde jumped up on the top of the wall and stood tall like a general commanding the others. "Attack!"

The demons scaled the wall and sat salivating, all in a row, like vultures waiting in a dead tree for an animal to die so they could begin their feast.

In the soft voice of my mother, the demon leader spoke. "Oh, my sweet, favorite little boy, you know how much I love you, how I cared for you. Can you simply toss away my dreams for you? Surely you won't because you have always been so special to me."

My mind fought what I knew was not real as my heart was drawn to expectations not mine.

I stood and screamed, "Go back to Hell from whence you came!" I fell to the ground, writhing in agony as the remaining unholy creatures of every unnatural form scratched and squeezed out of the pores of my skin. They reeked like sickly, toxic sweat.

The demon throng scampered over the wall like scared dogs, snapping at each other, leaving a trail of blood. It was mine, blood they exacted as tribute for their leader who, still standing on the wall, smirked like this skirmish was simply a minor setback in the great battle for my soul.

The mouth of the perfectly round gray rock gaped twice as wide as before. A great tongue like that of a frog snatched the demon leader from his perch on the wall the Great Voice had created to hold all my wrong emotions and thoughts at bay. I would have been devoured by the demons had not Creator provided that protection.

The demon leader shrieked as he and his horde were slowly swallowed by the large, perfectly round gray rock. "We will be back for you, for you are not strong."

I shouted, "But Creator is." The power within seized my soul as the large, perfectly round gray rock's great mouth closed shut.

The Golden Mansion of Happy Chaos I had lived in for so long returned to its dilapidated state, and the thousand faces that were mine had disappeared.

The Great Voice encouraged me. "*A memory to turn away from but never to forget.*"

"How could I have lived there for so long?"

"*You became content in that place.*"

"How could I?"

"*You gave up.*"

I fell to my knees, exhausted, but the ground on which I knelt was soft as an ancient padded prayer stand. For the first time in a long time, I felt safe and protected behind the great wall. "I am free to be me."

The old monk's face reappeared on the perfectly round gray rock that now sat on top of the wall. "You are very close to the bottom of the abyss. Stay alert, for It will be waiting and watching."

The large, gray rock rolled along the wall like a sentinel guarding an ancient city.

"Where are you going, monk? I need you with me."

"I must oversee rebuilding other damaged places in the wall Creator began at your birth. I'm never far away. And neither are they." He pointed to the stones in the wall, each an angel with a different weapon to guard against every unhealthy thought and emotion that might attack my soul.

Love, joy, and peace swelled in my chest and overflowed like an artesian well with the taste of the sweetest spring water bubbling up from within the deepest part of a mountain.

"Now and forever, I will live only by the power of the One Who Knows Who I Am."

The Great Voice, in the sound of a thousand blasting trumpets, announced, "*It is done! You may now go forward in your search for Naomi.*"

What lies behind us and what lies before us are
small matters compared to what lies within us.

—Ralph Waldo Emerson

CHAPTER 51

The Test

Work in the invisible world at least as hard as you do in the visible.

—Rumi

I HAD FINALLY escaped the demons of my own making to stand strong in the power and knowledge of Creator's will for me.

I descended the remaining part of the gorge on a staircase intricately carved from one large sapphire. The stairs led into a beautiful garden filled with every flowering bush and fruit tree ever created. With each step, sparkling threads wove together to form new clothing on my body. I had forgotten I wasn't wearing any.

The Great Voice whispered, *"She will not recognize you without these."*

Each piece of clothing became a different variation of the agate Granny had given me. The threads moved about frantically, trying to be the first to be threaded through the sewer's needle. Though nothing was written on them, I understood the meaning of the living strands as if words were inscribed on each one—goodness, compassion, acceptance, kindness, presence, love, and the list continued to grow with each new thread swirling around my body. When the last piece of my new apparel was affixed, the agate in my hand faded into my heart, and my new clothes glowed like a flickering bright candle in a deep cavern. The power of the clothes of light clasped my body like flexible armor. *This must be what an angel of light feels like. Am I one?*

The Great Voice replied, *"Not yet. There is but one last test."*

For the first time since I started this journey, I felt ready for the challenge. "What is it? Please tell me."

No surprise—Creator gave no answer.

For a moment, my old heart wanted to freeze in fear, but the new power within flamed with the roar of a lion to chase it away.

I waited. I didn't know what to do, so I started walking. I wandered through dense, sweet-smelling forests for hours on a path not of my choosing. I had to obey and go the way I was shown. The trail formed before me one short stretch at a time as I listened to the new prompts guiding me—healthy feelings and thoughts. I was on the best life path I'd followed in years, like how it was after being baptized at eleven years old. I enjoyed every new sensation, like someone was always near, watching me, leading me. Fear could not have been further from my soul.

Out of the shade of the tall trees, I walked into a green field covered with millions of tiny purple flowers dancing and singing, *"The One Who Frees comes to release."*

A lone tree stood in the middle, branches outstretched in a grandmotherly sort of way, softly and invitingly calling me.

I picked up my pace. "This must be the way." For some reason, I became more ravenous than I could ever remember. I was famished, and my hunger increased as the path faded. In a matter of moments, I could see the tree, but the path disappeared.

I stopped. "I know what to do." I formed a path in my mind, and it appeared, one of my own making. My desire to get to the tree became so strong, I started running with all the speed I could muster. I stopped short at the base of the beautiful tree that had brightly colored, delicious looking, low hanging fruit within easy reach. I was starving, and these were readily within my grasp.

I studied the tree and its fruit for a moment, and the face of my first grade Bible class teacher formed on each of the leaves. "Forget not the teaching when you became aware." Then, her face disappeared.

The bark on the tree changed into alligator skin and started moving, alive and slithering like so many snakes.

I gasped. "The Great Serpent."

His body, made of millions of writhing, venomous snakes, hissed and struck at me.

I tried to step back but couldn't move, like my feet were stuck in concrete.

"One in the same, old friend," the Great Serpent hissed. "I knew you'd be back."

Then, the most seductive female voice I'd ever heard tickled my ear. "Just look at the fruit for a while. Admire its color, its beauty, but don't taste it. Not just yet."

I couldn't take my eyes from its perfect roundness, its obvious luscious juiciness. My hunger became insatiable. I was like a vampire in an old movie, rising from my coffin, having not fed on the blood of others for days. I was losing control of my desire to grab the fruit and devour it.

The longer I stared at the fruit, the more the slithering bark reached out ever so slowly to engulf me, tightening its coils around my soul. The slimy beast wrapped around me, but I still couldn't take my eyes from the fruit or stop my mouth from salivating. The more the serpent's gentle voice persuaded, the more I wanted the fruit. My body shriveled with starvation as I reached for the beautifully ripened sphere of sweet goodness.

A quiet word touched my ear like the flicker of a snake's tongue. "Only the Fruit of Human Choice can satisfy your every hunger. Touch It, only for a moment. Stroke Its beautiful skin. I promise It won't hurt you, but It will satisfy your every longing. It will never let you die. It will make you feel alive again. It will give you power."

I wanted to pluck the fruit and devour it as quickly as I could, more than anything else I'd ever wanted in my life. I wanted It.

I glanced around like a child about to steal a cookie before supper. I touched the fruit, and immediately visions of all things I ever wanted exploded in my mind like multicolored confetti ribbons racing in all directions. Sensations of the ecstasy of satisfaction and contentment rolled up and down my body. I shuddered and felt weak from exhausting pleasure. Words appeared on each wave of delight, trying to convince me taking a bite of the fruit would supply everything I needed for my quest and more. A new and different power emerged within, stronger than ever. I knew things I shouldn't have but treasured the thoughts. I stood up straight, impressed with myself, ready to pluck the Fruit of Human Choice.

The charming voice continued, "You will be The All. You will be the wisest of all men. Nothing from you will be withheld, except only the one you cannot because you need not."

I paid no attention to the seducer's words. I wanted the fruit so badly, I would give up anything to taste it. Even my soul.

The Great Serpent slowly worked its way around the tree and my body until its face was inches from mine. My body and the tree were merging into one. I couldn't escape the grip of the tree, though I didn't try very hard. Scales like those of the Great Serpent formed on my arms.

I was becoming one with the Great Serpent.

"The power to save your daughter is before you. Just taste the fruit."

A thousand pleasant memories flashed before my eyes like on an old movie screen—some that didn't look familiar.

The Great Serpent whispered, "No need to worry, those are new memories you have created to replace the old ones that have no purpose here. Forget them. They only bring pain. You can now choose how you want to remember your life with Naomi. Always happy, always treating her well, always blissful, no matter what really happened. It cares not for what really happened. Remember the past how you want It to be. You have the power now. It will supply all your heart's desires."

I became drowsy. I wanted to sleep. I wanted to simply fade into nothingness.

I touched the fruit again, and the strength of a hundred men filled my arms and legs. The strength I experienced was like when, as a young man, I nearly killed a man in rage.

I held my fists up. "I like this anger. I am powerful. I can do anything."

Fearlessness stoked the fire burning rage in my heart. I held onto the fruit and couldn't turn it loose. I didn't want to. I wanted to see all things. The more I hungered, the more I lusted. The more pride swelled in my chest, the more the face of the serpent slowly became mine. Then, it was like looking into a mirror. My knees buckled.

The tongue of the Great Serpent tickled my ear. "The person who knows all has no fear except to inflict it upon others. Your power will overcome all. Just taste the fruit, and you will truly see."

The Great Serpent's eyes became like mirrors, enabling me to look intently into my own. The pupils changed from round to elliptical. Scales had replaced my skin, and the shape of my head narrowed as my ears receded. I felt like a mouse about to be swallowed by its fanged captor—helpless.

From the corner of my eye, a flicker of light blinked once. The agate stone Granny had given me came to mind. She whispered, "Even cockle burrs look beautiful until they attach. Then, they are loyal to a fault."

The Great Serpent laughed. "Go ahead, heed the old woman's words. I'm the best friend you'll ever have."

Granny held up the agate that had fallen to the ground from my heart. It glowed for a second.

It was enough. I shook my reptilian head and hissed with what little human voice I had left. "No. I've done this before, and look where it got me. The fault of which she speaks is mine."

Something wiggled in the pocket of my new clothes. I pulled out a beautiful piece of fruit just like the ones hanging on the tree. I held it tightly in my hand. It was alive, trying to return to my pocket.

"How did that get in there?"

I looked again at the mirror eyes that looked like mine.

The Great Serpent's face became that of the most seductively beautiful woman I'd ever seen. Her lips dripped with the sweet juiciness of the fruit that could satisfy my every appetite. "You will regret your choice to not make your own decisions. You will never be happy surrendering your will to another. Just one small bite from the Fruit of Human Choice, and happiness will forever be yours."

I studied the tree and found a small branch within reach that had lost its fruit. My name was written on the stem in small, barely legible letters. I caressed the fruit I held in my hand.

The Great Serpent leaned closer. "That's *It*, keep going. Doesn't that feel good? *It* will taste even better."

I looked up at the fruit still attached to the tree. I hesitated.

"It's okay, you can take another. Then, you will have two. You'll be doubly powerful in all things. What could stop you from getting your daughter back now? You are strong and wise to plot your own path. How could you go wrong?"

I thought back to the first time I lied to my parents. It was happening all over again. This was the greatest lie—believing I possessed the wisdom to chart my own course when I had no idea of what it might lead to.

The Great Serpent was crafty. He had both of my hands occupied. One with the fruit of the past, the other with the fruit of the future. As hard as I tried, I couldn't release my grip. I was trapped and couldn't find my present time, *the now*.

Naomi's face appeared faintly on one very small leaf next to the fruit on the tree I held in my hand. The Great Serpent ferociously devoured it.

My first grade Bible class teacher's words returned. "If you take *It*, *It* will always be yours."

"What else can I do?"

The Great Serpent rounded the tree like a freight train barreling out of control down the tracks. The friction singed my new clothes.

The Great Voice spoke at just the right moment. *"You know."*

In one swift motion, I let go of the fruit on the Tree of Human Choice and reattached the fruit from my pocket to the stem that bore my name.

The Great Serpent hissed and struck at me as it frantically circled the tree. "You can't do that. You must keep it once you removed it from the tree."

"That's where you're wrong, O Great Serpent. If I chose to take the fruit from the Tree of Human Choice, then I can choose to give it back. You old trickster, I no longer want the power to decide what is right and wrong, to choose the path of my life. Here and now, I surrender every thought of self-will to my Creator."

The Great Voice sighed in relief.

I looked to the sky. "Into your hands I commit my spirit, Creator."

"This is my son, in whom I am well pleased."

The earth shook as the Great Serpent with the beautiful woman's face circled the tree in flashes of lightning and peals of thunder.

The Great Voice called to me. *"Because you have chosen the One Who Lives Within, free will can now guide your every step."*

The fruit on the Tree of Human Choice withered to a rotting, foul-smelling prune of its former beauty, then fell from the tree. When it hit the ground at my feet, a thousand maggots poured out of its core, each with a different desire that had taken me away from the true path I had known to follow all along. I watched it dissolve as if it had never existed. Not even a stain on the ground was left.

The Great Voice thundered in the dark clouds that had formed over me. *"To taste the fruit is to become the fruit."*

I shuddered at the thought that for years I had taken my life into my own hands.

The beautiful face of the woman in the slithering bark returned to that of a great fanged snake. The tree shook and twisted as if in a great tornado. My new clothes were being torn from my body by the wicked gale force winds of the Great Serpent's fiery, wrathful breath. All the good Creator had brought me so far was fading before my eyes.

Roots from the Tree of Human Choice erupted from the dirt as countless snakes. They trapped my feet and chained them to the ground. The Great Serpent writhed in agony, striking this way and that, like he was on fire. He stopped suddenly and glared at me with eyes blazing red. His penetrating gaze froze me like a statue. It slowly opened its mouth to swallow me.

I couldn't run or defend myself. "Please. This can't be the end of me and Naomi. Please help, I'm begging you." Those feeble mumbles were all I could manage.

In a flash of lightning, a flaming gold sword wielded by a being dressed in robes of rainbow light pounced on the back of the beast. Slashing the Great Serpent with every turn, the Being of Light drove it out of the tree and into the ground.

My feet were freed. I stumbled backward, fell to the ground, then fainted.

I woke to the Being of Light with the Great Sword standing over me, scanning all directions at once with a thousand faces searching for more lurking enemies.

I collected myself. "Who are you?"

"The People's Protector."

"Thank you."

"No need to thank me. Truth of my existence comes with the power."

"Power?"

"Creator endows power within those who use it only to protect others. The Great Serpent never understood that."

"I don't know what to do next."

In the voice of a drill sergeant, the People's Protector snapped, "How many times must you be told the same thing? Be who Creator made you to be."

"How do I do that?"

"Have you forgotten?"

"Did I ever know?"

"You did when you surrendered years ago."

"Surrendered when?"

"At your second birth."

"Why did I need a second birth?"

"You gave away the first birth when you tasted the fruit."

"I just gave it back."

"I saw."

"It was difficult."

"I know."

"I could have lived without the pains of all I did to harm Naomi."

"You would have forgotten her, and she would have been forever lost. Is that what you want?"

"No."

"Then only you can choose *It*."

"So, that's *It*?"

"Now you understand."

"Where do I go?"

"Go where you choose. It will guide you."

"What do I do next?"

"Find the Name Tree."

The People's Protector vanished along with the once beautiful tree with its tasty fruit.

I was alone but never felt more surrounded with power to do what I needed to continue. "I can make the right choice now because I don't have to." My body shook, and all the air was sucked from my lungs. Scales fell from my arms. My face returned to normal. I could breathe again. My breath smelled of honey.

A great cheer arose from a stadium filled with thousands of people who had been watching from above. It was like I'd won an Olympic gold medal. My clothes shone as bright as the sun.

The Great Voice complimented me. *"Out of your victory, the gold of the Universe is created, my son."* My new clothes were restored. *"Wear them well and never forget whose name you wear."*

The path not of my choosing returned. I started for the forest ahead. I knew exactly where I was going.

———————————

When the right spirit walks in, the wrong spirits get nervous.

—Unknown

PART TWELVE

The Tree

If you want something you never had
then you have to do something you've never done.

—Unknown

CHAPTER 52

The No-Name Tree

Even the darkest night will end and the sun will rise.

—*Victor Hugo*

A FOREST OF very large and tall trees shed rainbow leaves that swirled in small twisters. Birds of every kind flocked to fill the branches, matching their various hues. It was difficult to tell the leaves from the birds. They were all so striking. Though no two tunes were alike, they sang more beautifully than any human chorus I'd ever heard, praising Creator in perfect unison in a myriad of different harmonies.

"Is this what it was like in the beginning?"

The trees swayed in the gentle breeze, singing, *"It was, it was, it always was."*

An old withered sign that looked a thousand years old read, "Trees That Reach for the Limitless Sky." With no end to their branches' reach, the tips of their leaves blended with clouds floating in a sky that changed color with each new breeze.

"I'm in the right place. I must be close to the Name Tree."

From out of nowhere, claws of fear grappled for my heart.

"I don't have what it takes to enter this forest."

The leaves and birds stopped then sang one tune. *"You are not alone. You are not alone."*

The Great Voice sighed in exasperation. *"You're right. You don't have enough strength, or even the wisdom, to find The Tree That Bears Her Name. You never did. You never had to."*

I touched my chest where the agate stone lay. The claws retreated.

I found a small opening through The Trees That Reach for the Limitless Sky. They stood so tightly packed together I had to turn sideways to pass. They moved to make it difficult for me to squeeze through, like they were guarding something very precious. The deeper in I went, the bolder their trunks became, swaying back and forth, nearly flattening me like a pancake. A bird the size and color of a small agate appeared just head of me, guiding me through the dense woods. I followed the small bird to a light that flickered between the trees.

The large trunks gave way to a valley encircled with every kind of flowering tree ever created. Their fragrances blended in a scent beyond what I'd ever enjoyed. I closed my eyes and savored a moment of rest from my trek. Then, I looked about. Wonderful fragrances dripped from the trees in an unstoppable flow of tears shed for a withered, leafless old trunk that stood under a circling gray cloud in the center of the field.

"Is that the Name Tree?"

The Great Voice whistled from a flock of green and yellow parakeets that flew by. *"Only you can know."*

I ran to the great tree, felt its smooth, gray bark, and searched every inch for Naomi's name. It was not there. I whimpered. I cried. I wailed. But I never stopped examining every blemish and knothole. I couldn't find the letters I'd carved on the tree so long ago. There was no name on the Name Tree.

I sat down, bewildered and defeated. "But I've come so far."

"Have you?"

"What is this, the No-Name Tree?"

The Great Voice from inside the tree said, *"Be still in the place assigned to you."*

I leaned back against the Name Tree between two great exposed roots smoother than polished marble. Exhausted from my journey, I dozed.

A tiny beam of light warmed my eyelids, and I woke to a faint chirping.

A small sparrow sang happily as she hopped from one of my knees to the other. "Creator cares for the least of these, as Creator cares for me."

"I am in the right place." I slipped into a deep sleep, too tired to dream.

Silence my soul,
these trees are prayers.
I asked the tree,
"Tell me about God,"
Then it blossomed.

—Rabindranath Tagore

CHAPTER 53

Finding Naomi

Emotions are like waves. Watch them disappear
in the distance on the vast calm of the ocean.

—*Ram Dass*

I AWOKE TO a whimper, like a young child lost and crying. I peeked over the large, gray exposed root on my left to see a small, blonde girl in a sack dress, shivering. She covered her face with her hands and constantly shifted her feet back and forth like she was walking but going nowhere.

There sat eleven-year-old Naomi in the shade of the withered tree with smooth, gray bark. She peeked out from behind her hands but covered her eyes as quickly as she had uncovered them.

I wanted to wrap her in my arms and never let go, but I was afraid she might run if I moved. I wanted to shout for joy yet wanted to be still as a mouse, both extremes at once. Then, I remembered. She will not survive the imbalance of my emotions.

I meditated for a moment, emptying my soul. I re-balanced my thoughts with my emotions so I could think more clearly. I quieted my fears and contained my joy. It's what she needed me to do. The agate

Granny had given me glowed as I calmed my spirit. Finally, I was doing the right thing—what was best for her—instead of feeding my empath need.

I softly called, "Naomi."

At the sound of my voice, Naomi cocked her head, turning one ear toward me. Her puzzled expression indicated she was trying to figure out who was talking. I had hoped when I found her, even if she didn't know her name, she would at least recognize me.

She didn't.

Not at first.

As she looked curiously in my direction with a blank stare, she mouthed the word, "Dad?" She was lost like a little lamb caught in a bush of demon claws grasping and clawing to keep her confused and disoriented.

I quietly stood. I wanted to cry but instead planted my feet and clenched my fists, ready to do battle with whatever or whoever came at me. I would save my little girl.

Convinced we were alone for the moment, I realized where I was and why. I had found Naomi cowered beside a withered dying tree bearing a sign with words written in blood.

I killed myself, and now I am nobody.

I wilted like a rose in desert heat. I wanted to fall down crying, but it was not the time. I carefully touched Naomi's shoulder.

She shrunk back in fear. "No. No. Please, just leave me alone."

I didn't remove my hand, hoping the power within me, not mine, would calm her spirit.

She looked up with a slight grin, her eyes glassed over like those of a blind person.

I wailed without sound for a moment but collected myself quickly. She didn't need my pain. She just kept searching for the source of my voice.

She tried to get up, but her legs were like those of an emaciated Holocaust victim, just skin and bones. She leaned back, lifeless, and quietly spoke. "I am not a victim. I help victims." Then, she fell asleep.

When Naomi was twenty, she had accompanied me on a church mission trip to Ukraine for a month. On one of our breaks, we visited two World War II concentration camps, Auschwitz and Birkenau, where thousands had been slaughtered simply for being who Creator made them to be.

After witnessing the gas chamber and ovens where so many were murdered, Naomi became completely overwhelmed with horror. When we moved away from the pits where the Nazis had dumped the ashy remains of their victims, she said, "There's something I have to do."

Without another word, she walked the entire length of the tracks leading from where the victims exited the trains all the way to the front gate of the prison. It was as if she floated along, purposefully reliving each Holocaust victim's terror and death. When we reached the gate, she collapsed, taking on the pain of the thousands who had died there.

Naomi died a thousand deaths that day. I should have known then that the pains of our world were and would always be too much for her.

I sat beside lost little Naomi as she rested her back against the great withered tree's gray bark. She looked right and left, sensing my presence, until she found my place.

I stroked her disheveled hair and wiped her tearstained cheeks.

Her lips formed the word, "Dad?"

This time, there was sound.

You don't have a soul. You are a soul. You have a body.

—*C.S. Lewis*

PART THIRTEEN
A Promise Kept

Creator spoke, "I am in All. All is in Me.
I give purpose to All. I hold All together."
I asked, "So, what does that make me?"
"Irreplaceable Purpose."
"How can that be?"
"Child, I took a pinch of Myself. I contemplated timeless meaning.
I tossed the seed into the universe and declared, 'You!'"

—the author

I looked intently into her swirling agate eyes
and saw a window back into my soul.
In that moment, Creator opened me
to the oneness of the Universe.

—the author

CHAPTER 54

Sitting with Naomi

The human face is the icon of creation.

—John O'Donohue

NAOMI AND I talked for hours, laughing and crying, telling old stories, good and not so good. I confessed the wrongs I'd done against her, especially the time I said she had a bad heart and the other when I didn't let her sit in my lap when she needed my comfort. A mourning dove called as I finished. I wanted to make it up to her somehow.

A flock of small green and yellow parakeets passed by whistling, "She knows your heart."

She looked at me with eyes that had yet to become completely clear and read my thoughts. "You can't, Dad. But you don't have to."

"Thank you," was all I could choke out through the lump in my throat.

Naomi's eyes cleared as she looked right, then left. "I don't know where I am, Dad, and I don't know what to do. What is my name? I can't remember."

I couldn't help it. I cried.

She patted me on the back. "It's all right. You know my name. That's why you're here, isn't it? To tell me my name?"

I nodded, wiping away tears. "To help you find it, yes, but not to tell you. You must find your name. When you do, it will be truly yours."

"I knew you'd come for me, Dad. You kept your promise."

"I had to." I wept like a child losing his mother. My chest heaved, and I gasped for breath. I'd never cried so hard. I nearly fainted away.

Naomi put her arm around me. "It's okay. We're together again, and you're here to help me."

A glint of gold flashed in the corner of my eye from above. There on a shriveled drooping limb hung a pomegranate made of gold.

I looked around. "Is it okay to take the fruit?"

It immediately fell from the tree into my cupped hands.

Naomi reached and took it. "I love these. They're my favorite." She polished the pomegranate until its husk fell from the thousand glowing red seeds dazzling in the faint light. She carefully pulled each fleshy seed coat from the pomegranate of gold and popped it in her mouth. She savored the juice and swallowed its seed. With each seed consumed, Naomi's strength and clarity of mind returned.

The tree sprouted new green leaves, and small, purple flowers budded. Its trunk and limbs were no longer withered. Naomi was returning to her former self, and as she did, the beauty of the tree was restored.

"I never knew where I was going or who I was, Dad."

"Oh, baby, I'm so sorry. That was my fault. I should've been there to help you. I was so busy saving other people that I failed to help you. Please forgive me."

Her silence was as thick as the sweet smell of lavender enveloping our space. The sky suddenly went a soft purple. Naomi's favorite color.

"How can I not forgive you? You're my father."

"I didn't know if you would."

"SHE didn't have all power over me just because SHE gave birth to me." It was the strongest statement I'd ever heard Naomi make.

"I'm glad."

"You came for me when no one else would, Dad."

"I had to, Naomi. My good friend said the reason you didn't leave me a farewell letter was because you knew I'd come for you. Is that true?"

"I always knew you would come because you told me that the day we found the…." She couldn't remember.

"Let's stand up, okay?" I had to pull her to her feet. Her legs were like that of a newborn fawn, weak and wobbly. I steadied her until she could stand on her own.

Other pomegranates of gold formed on the tree and sang words to a beautiful tune I didn't recognize. Naomi sang with them as she popped the glowing red seeds into her mouth. As she danced with the music, a small pen with a fiery tip etched each letter of her name into the smooth, gray bark that had become a great old beech tree.

"I've never heard that song before. Where did you learn it?"

"I wrote the words and music for it, but it hasn't been created."

"Why not?"

"The person I was supposed to become hasn't written it yet."

"You will now."

A tiny bolt of lightning in the shape of a quill filled each letter in Naomi's name with liquid gold.

I gently led her hand to the spot where we had carved her name into the beech tree so many years ago.

Though she didn't recognize the word yet, the warmth left by the fiery pen made her smile. "Is that my name?"

Before I could answer, a loud, reptilian howl thundered beneath our feet.

Naomi snapped her head around. The ground around us churned like a giant mole digging through the earth faster than a subway train in a tunnel. She shuddered uncontrollably, like she expected any moment to be swallowed by some approaching deadly predator.

As light gathered around the Name Tree, Naomi's eyes dazzled like blue sapphires. She stared directly into my eyes, piercing my soul.

My knees buckled. *Will she run away?*

The Lord said to Satan, "Where have you come from?"
Satan answered the Lord, "From roaming throughout the earth,
going back and forth on it."

—Job 1:7, NIV

CHAPTER 55

A Golden Heart

For our soul sits in God in true rest,
and our soul stands in God in sure strength,
and our soul is naturally rooted in God in endless love.

—*Julian of Norwich*

A DARK SHADOW clawed from the earth with a deafening roar. Thunder clashed as a hideous beast flapped its mighty wings and swooped overhead, screeching with the cry of ten thousand demons. Darkness dimmed the light surrounding the tree.

"We have to hide. Now, Dad." Naomi grabbed a golden pomegranate and ducked down into her hiding place between the smooth, gray roots of the tree now healed. Tiny, frightened, crying faces—all Naomi's— formed on the golden pomegranates.

I planted my feet in front of the tree with my daughter shivering behind me and faced the Great Serpent circling high in the sky. His face was that of a menacing vulture ready to consume a fresh carcass. When he landed, some of the golden pomegranates shook loose. Scaly arms sprouted from his wings, and he began snatching at all of the fallen fruit of Naomi's new life to come. The tiny faces on the golden pomegranates shrieked and screamed as the Great Serpent shoved a handful into his mouth.

I flexed my muscles, drawing on the power within, and called out, "Stop! Give them back."

The Great Serpent spat the fruit back into his clawed hand. His footsteps thundered and shook the earth as he marched toward me. "I will not, you frightened little man."

"That's where you're wrong, Old Dragon. I no longer live in $\phi OBO\sum$."

"No. You cannot know that word." The Great Serpent's forked tongue stretched to snatch the golden pomegranates of Naomi's talents and gifts with his scaly hand.

"I live in the strength of the Great Voice."

As the Great Serpent put the handful of fruit to his mouth to swallow them all, the People's Protector raced across the sky with the great golden sword, slashing this way and that, to chase the cursing demon away from the branches of the tree, sending him back into the abyss.

The People's Protector landed beside me with force of an earthquake. "He will not return."

I gently took Naomi by the shoulders. "It's okay. The Great Serpent is gone. It's me, your dad."

She blinked twice like she had awakened from a long dream. "Why are you here? I don't remember."

"I had to come. I love you."

"But I never really felt that before, Dad."

My heart sank. The pain in those words was almost more than I could bear. Old memories flooded my mind, and anger filled my heart at myself. Tears welled, but this was not the time. *Remember, she won't survive your imbalance.*

"I know that, sweetheart. Please forgive me." I put my arm around her and we cried.

Naomi wiped her tears, then reached to wipe mine. "I know you love me. You loved me even back then. I was taught not to forgive you, Dad. But SHE no longer controls me. SHE who gave birth to many things not good."

I didn't say anything.

Naomi looked up into the sky. "I don't know who I am here."

"It's because you didn't really know who you were then."

"Why am I here?"

"I didn't love you as you deserved." I cried until blood dripped from my eyes.

"What's my name again, Dad? I'm confused."

"Remember, I can't tell you. You must find it for yourself." I took her hand and placed it again on the letters burned in the beech tree bark by the lightning pen.

She started with the N and stopped at each letter, feeling the still-warm gold in the smooth, gray bark. She stared at them for several moments.

"Remember wandering in the woods with me that day when you were eleven? We carved those same letters into the bark of the great old beech tree so we would never forget our special place that only you and I could visit."

"You didn't forget me, did you, Dad?"

"No, and I never will."

Her eyes glassed over again, and she closed them for a moment. I could feel her absorbing the power—not mine—from within me. When she opened her eyes, the air was thick with the scent of roses and flowers that sprang up around us. They were the color of deep blue sapphires to match her eyes. She met my gaze without blinking, and my eyes ached from the intensity of the blue flames sparkling around her pupils. I would not look away.

While running three fingers over the letters, she smiled. She understood. One after another, she gave voice to each letter. "N-A-O-M-I." For a moment, she hesitated, then she began to sound out the name like a kid learning words in first grade. "Is that my name? Naomi?"

"Yes!" I shouted. I danced and jumped up and down.

Naomi stared at me curiously because I'd never done that before. "And you're my dad." She got up, then we danced like we did at her wedding. She sang like she did so many times in church. She laughed like she used to when she made fun of the ragged sweatpants and hiking boots I'd wear to the grocery store just to embarrass her. Naomi returned to herself.

I shouted to the heavens, "She knows me!" I thought my heart would burst with joy.

Something started glowing like a tiny ember through her sack dress. The small light became brighter and brighter. She looked down and grinned. The glow took the shape of a heart of gold. "See, Dad, I do have a good heart."

"You always did, sweetheart. My blind eyes just wouldn't let me see it."

"I forgive you."

I could say nothing for a long time. I sat to take it all in.

Naomi pushed my arm aside and gently sat on my lap. She put her arms around my neck. I wanted to stay there with her forever. She eased into a peaceful slumber. I leaned my head back against the tree, recounting all I had experienced thus far.

A gentle touch shook my shoulder. I awakened to Granny in her gown of multicolored, living agate. "Your rest is done. You two must follow me." Granny disappeared down a new path that swirled like the robe she wore.

Naomi awoke with a start and stood. She gazed down the path, straining to see what was ahead. "Who was that?" Without waiting for my answer, she stepped back and examined the tree with her name carved in big letters. "This was it, wasn't it?"

I nodded. "Yes."

"It was our special place."

"It still can be if you want it to be."

"How?"

"Oh, there's just a sheer veil between the seen and unseen if you find just the right thin spot."

"How do you know that?"

Immediately, new green leaves budded out to their full length on the limbs of the Name Tree. It was beautiful, like it was when Creator first planted it there. Granny's smiling face appeared in the smooth bark of the great old beech tree just below Naomi's carved name.

"A wise and ancient woman taught me those things when I was but a child." I smiled back at Granny, then she disappeared into the tree.

"Who was she, Dad?"

"Someone who has known you since before you were born."

Naomi placed her hand on the spot where Granny's face had been. Light emanated from the bark through her hand to fill her golden heart. "That was Granny, wasn't it?"

"Yes. How'd you know?"

"I've seen her before."

"How? When?"

"She came to me and put something into my pocket." Naomi reached into the only pocket on her sack dress. She pulled out a bright, multicolored agate, then held it up for me to see.

I was taken back. We sat, and I told her all about my petite great-grandmother who stood just four feet eleven inches and wore only a size three shoe yet was a formidable force for good in our family.

"Had it not been for Granny, I could not have found you. She has been the guide to keep me on course."

Naomi placed her hand on the tree. "Thank you, Great-great-grandmother." The agate stone glowed with all its colors, and swirls flowed from the rock into Naomi's golden heart. She stood like she was ready to run.

Naomi gazed down the path where Granny disappeared. "Dad, it's time to go. That's the way." She pulled me up.

I shook the dust of a thousand bad memories from my clothes—the dust of a thousand things done wrong now forgiven. I let the dust fall where it landed and didn't look back.

"Let's go find where you're supposed to be." I took Naomi's hand.

She started to step then pulled me to a stop. "No, there's one thing left to do."

"What's that?"

"We must give this place a name, one we will remember."

"What is the best thing you are taking with you as we leave?"

"My name."

"Exactly."

Naomi grinned. "Okay then, we'll call it… *the Name Tree*."

"Perfect."

She thought for moment. "That's what we used to call it, wasn't it?"

I nodded as we stood underneath the Name Tree hand in hand.

A sign with an arrow appeared in the middle of the road. It read, "The Path to Peace Begins Here." I said nothing but knew all the demons that opposed Naomi's ascent would find their way here, too. But we had to go forward. There was no turning back. And Naomi now knew her name.

She straightened her sack dress and, like a trumpet releasing an army to go do battle, announced, "I'm ready. Let's go." She clutched my hand. "Follow me. I've traveled this path before."

Our first step together was greeted with a smothering, twisting blast from the furnace where I'd first seen Naomi. Hot, suffocating, straight-line winds blew us both down.

We picked ourselves up, then dusted off the smoldering cinders.

I saw a touch of fear mixed with determination in Naomi's eyes. "This will not be easy. Will it, Dad?"

"Not in this place, but it'll be worth the struggle."

"I'm not afraid."

"Why's that?"

"You're here with me."

That was all I needed to hear. I squeezed her hand.

She braced herself and took a step onto The Path to Peace Begins Here.

———————————

The best way out is always through.

—*Robert Frost*

CHAPTER 56

No Time to Rest

Even the smallest thought or act of love resets the Universe.

—the author

A CAVE WITH many tunnels opened in a mountain that dropped from the sky. They looked familiar, but I didn't know which to choose. A twinge of fear crept into my soul.

Naomi looked up at me and shuddered. "Dad, I know this place. I've stood at the edge of the deep part of my soul many times but was too afraid to look in, much less walk in. I didn't want to be ashamed or let you down."

"You have never let me down."

Naomi stood frozen like a statue, gazing into the dark halls of her troubled soul. "I don't want to now."

"Are you okay?"

"Not really. These are the caverns of my life, not yours. I'll have to guide us through as I walk around in my own soul. But you must help me get through to the other side. I can't do it alone. I've tried." She looked at me for reassurance.

"I'll be by your side all the way."

We both touched our chests where the agates Granny had given us lay.

"There." Naomi pointed to a flicker of rainbow light escaping through a thin passageway.

Holding each other's hands tightly, we took a few small steps through the cavernous maze of winding paths and diverting trails. The walls came alive with demons I had allowed into my heart that had worked their wickedness on Naomi.

"I'm scared." Naomi shrunk back at the hideous mass of writhing angry demons gnashing their teeth at us and each other. They cursed and clawed at me.

"I know. I need to stop for a minute."

"Are you all right, Dad?"

"Yeah, for the most part. You don't know it, but those are the demons of all the wrong things I did that hurt you and the family. The Great Serpent wants me to give up and turn back like I've done too many times before."

Naomi touched her agate heart. "It's okay. As long as we have the light in these stones of the universe, we'll be okay."

"Let me rest for a moment. The demons have just about done me in."

"That helps me understand better what happened to you when you were little, Dad."

"They're so strong, but I did choose to let them into my soul."

Naomi shuddered and shrunk back from the demon horde surrounding us. "Some things you didn't ask for though."

"True, but don't think I blame them for my worst thoughts and deeds. No, for whatever reason, in my weakness, I let them in. And we were all the worse for it."

"That must've been agonizing."

"I want to say, 'you have no idea,' but I know you do."

Naomi tightened her grip on my hand and waited until I was ready to go forward.

I figured this was as good a time as any to get off my chest what I'd wanted to say for a long time. "Naomi, I allowed these insidious creatures of the Great Serpent to take me into places only demons dared. I allowed myself to do things I could not justify before Creator or my family. I justified bad thoughts and actions, believing a little sin would be all right because I was such a great servant of Creator. I thought I deserved it. I told myself I could stop anytime I wanted. So, I became what they wanted me to be, that which I had chosen to be. The double life I led took you to the place of no return when you took your life."

Naomi pulled me close. "I've already told you I love you and forgive you. Why won't you accept it?"

I knew the answer but didn't want to say it. But I did. "I never learned to love myself."

"That's it. That's what the agate stone Granny gave me has been whispering into my soul since we left the Name Tree."

I touched my chest where my agate stone lay. "I was told for so long that I was worthless and no good, heard it so much I came to believe it. That's when I let the demons in. The pain of doing their bidding was far less than what I carried. At least, I thought so."

"Well, they're not in there now."

It hit me like a ton of bricks. I had been freed of the demons a while back but still held onto what no longer gripped my soul. Except by my choice.

The Great Voice spoke. "They could have been gone long ago had you only believed."

Naomi looked all around. "I know that voice. Whose is it?"

"The one who knows you the best and loves you the most—Creator."

"Then Creator knows you and loves you, too, Dad."

I screamed, "Be gone!"

The demons on the walls disappeared in a wisp of smoke.

Naomi took my jaw in her hand and made me look into her eyes. "Listen to me. I don't know what all is up ahead or what it will be like when we get there. But I do know this. There are parts of you and parts of me that could not be fixed until we got here, on the other side. However this ends, we will be better for it."

"Okay." This was the true Naomi I knew. The strong, caring, intelligent soul living deep inside the troubled young woman who became so hopeless that she took her life.

"And if I took my life, then surely by the power within I can find it and get it back." Suddenly, Naomi matured from an eleven-year-old girl to the thirty-three year old woman she was at her death, more beautiful than ever.

I wrapped my arms around her. "You already have."

"Let's stay here for a little while, Dad."

A string of words bubbled out of my mouth, the poem I had written so long ago.

"I watched you sprout from nothingness
On the first day of spring when you arrived
Budding on the branch of a towering tree, I asked,
Were you always so beautiful in the mind of God?"

"Dad, where did that come from?"

"I don't know."

"It was beautiful. Was it about me?"

"Who else could it be about?"

She hugged me close. Immediately, the demons of her many pains turned loose and escaped to the ceiling and walls of the narrow cavern pathway like a swarm of insects. Their humming grew louder, like summer cicadas, with each beat of my heart. They scratched and clawed at us, striking us with stones. Then, the agate hearts in our chests shown like a bright spotlight, and the insect-like demons scampered away as fast as they could travel, screeching and cursing.

We emerged from the cavern relatively unscathed, only a few minor scratches and bruises scattered about. In front of us lay a canyon wall with narrow steps carved in an agate stone path leading upward.

Naomi looked at me. "That way?"

"Don't worry. We've done this before."

When the path ignites the soul,
there's no remaining in place.
The foot touches the ground,
but not for long.

—Hakim Sanai

PART FOURTEEN

The Ascent

To come to the knowledge you have not
You must go by a way in which you know not.

—*St. John of the Cross*

CHAPTER 57

Three Ascents up Holy Hill

Allow your wounds to make you into something better.

—the author

As Naomi and I left the darkness of the cave, the Great Voice thundered, *"Climb Holy Hill."*

We both turned back to see the Name Tree pulling itself up by the roots with its massive limbs. It slowly moved from its place at the end of a long-straightened tunnel large enough for a traveling locomotive.

Naomi and I looked at each other, then up at the great wall of the abyss that towered above us.

"Dad, I'm scared."

"Baby, I know. But we're not alone."

The Name Tree stood next to us, and the Great Voice spoke from its trunk. One limb pointed at me. *"You descended the Three into your abyss."* Another pointed at Naomi. *"You must ascend the Three from yours."*

Naomi shuddered like she was in a blistering snow storm.

I wrapped my arms around her.

"I don't think I can do this, Dad." She turned away to sit down by the Name Tree, her place of comfort and security, just like I had done so many times.

"You don't have to, Naomi."

The Great Voice spoke in the sound of rushing waters. *"Only together will you do this."* The Great Voice hummed a familiar tune as the Name Tree sprouted new leaves and bloomed flowers of every color and kind.

"Okay, Dad, I trust you." Those words put fire into my soul again.

The Name Tree shrunk to a size that would fit in a photograph and became a picture. I picked up the photo from the ground. The picture had my face next to the tree like the one I had taken of Naomi beside her name so many years ago. Only this time, it was my present face.

The letters of Naomi's name disappeared from the gray tree bark in the photo and reappeared on her right hand, tattooed in a beautiful script. She gently touched it, then placed her hand over her heart. Her clothes transformed into those she wore when we carved her name into the Name Tree—blue jeans, sweatshirt, and pink jacket.

"I know my name."

"Yes, you do."

"And I've climbed a big hill like this before?"

"Yes, with me."

She looked back through the tunnel where the Name Tree once stood. She touched the tattoo on her hand and smiled. "If Creator can do that, then I can climb this hill."

"Ain't no hill for a stepper, my great-grandpa used to say."

Naomi took a deep breath and grabbed my hand. "Time to go."

She who begins a path must trust the One waiting at the end.

—the author

CHAPTER 58

The Gate

The face that launched a thousand ships set her chosen city afire.

—the author

W E SPUN AROUND to find a large, intricately carved bronze door like the gate of an ancient city. The entrance was guarded by two beautiful Amazon-esque women, one with a bow and arrow, and the other a sword and spear. Each had an elaborately decorated shield behind them, leaning against the gate posts.

In opera-style voices, they announced in unison, "You have found the path to true beauty. We guard the door. Few find it. Few choose to pass through this gate. Few are allowed to enter."

The wall surrounding the great doors came to life as thousands of women, whose beauty was matchless but equally unique, brandished weapons of every kind in a defensive stance ready for battle.

I asked, "Who are they?"

The two answered, "These are those who found true beauty within."

"May we pass?" I asked.

"Do you have the tribute word that must be paid to enter?"

"Tribute word?" Naomi and I looked at each other trying to figure out what it could be.

The sentries spoke in unison, their voices like the sound of a great waterfall. "The answer comes only from within, a clear message from Creator."

I whispered to Naomi, "Do you know?"

Naomi started to shake her head, but I tilted mine in silent warning for her not to speak her thoughts aloud.

One guard stamped her spear on the ground as the other drew back her bow. "What is the word? You must say the word before you may pass."

"Wait, wait. I know this." I thought and thought. I back-tracked the entire journey to when I first saw Granny.

The sentinels stepped forward, ready for battle.

I fumbled for the answer, rubbing my head. "Please, just a minute. Oh, what did she say?"

They sang as they approached, "You must answer now or return from that which you came." They raised their weapons, poised to strike.

"No, no, no. I know it. It's the meaning of your name, Naomi." I straightened up, somewhat proud but more relieved, and announced, "*Pleasantness* will be yours."

The guards backed away. They laid their weapons down, then lifted the great metal bar that locked the huge gate. The great doors cracked and popped, having not been opened for ages.

In unison, they cried out, "You may enter."

As we started for the open doors, one handed me a small, golden shield with a living agate of a thousand colors in the center.

"Guide and Protect" was written on my shield.

The other handed Naomi a cup of cool water and a piece of bread. "Your fast is complete. Eat. This will sustain you." When Naomi had finished her meal, the sentry handed her a shield like the one I was given. "Never Forget" was written on hers.

Both guards looked at me with blazing eyes of blue flame. "You must do without to go within."

I understood. I must continue my fast. I couldn't let my mental capacities be distracted with food digestion.

They returned to their guardian stance, their silence a dismissal.

But I had to know. "Who are you, may I ask?"

"Those sent to serve the Inheritors."

"Angels?"

"If you wish to call us so, you may."

"Will you go with us?"

"We cannot. We can only assist with what your heart intends."

Naomi shuddered. "I'm scared, Dad."

"I know. But I am with you always."

The angels spoke again in unison. "Be not afraid, child, for your father goes before you."

Faithless is he that says farewell when the road darkens.

—J.R.R. Tolkien

CHAPTER 59
The First Ascent

Butterflies cannot see their wings. But the rest of the world can.
You. You are beautiful. While you may not see it, we can.

—Unknown

FTER NAOMI AND I entered, the gates slammed shut behind us with a loud clang. It was dark except for spotlights flashing here and there. They stopped for only a fraction of a second to illuminate mannequin-like women who all looked exactly alike, wearing the same expensive clothes and jewelry, the same beautifully done hair, the same perfect makeup, and the same plastered smiles that seemed slightly devious. They didn't move. They couldn't. They weren't real, but I recognized the look. Chills slithered up and down my back like a cold snake. They looked exactly like the women in Naomi's college sorority picture. I touched the agate stone, and it warmed me all over.

"Am I home, Dad?"

All the roaming lights became one great spotlight shining on Naomi. She was transformed to look just like others. She smiled and walked like a model showing off her look.

"No," I cried.

But the light shone brighter.

The women who all looked the same walked stiffly toward us, arms outstretched like robots to greet Naomi. The closer they came, the more frighteningly lifeless they became. Their smiles were painted on. Their eyes were blank.

I felt afraid and fearless, weak and strong, all in the same instant.

Naomi flailed around like she was off balance and couldn't steady herself. She was becoming plastic. The frightening mannequins' hands became claws that, if sunk into Naomi's flesh, could not be removed without killing her. I couldn't let that happen.

Naomi smiled with tears flowing. "I want to be with them, Dad, but I know I am not them."

I calmed myself down, controlling the turbulent changes in my emotions. I touched my agate stone, and suddenly the strength of a lion surged within.

Naomi steadied herself, and the mannequin women gasped with surprised, gaping mouths. She tore at the clothes that hid her true spiritual apparel. She no longer wanted the clothes of her former self. She frantically rubbed off the caked-on makeup.

I blocked the blinding spotlight with the shield the angel had given me.

Naomi collapsed, exhausted from trying to free herself from the power of wanting to be desirable. I laid her shield over her body.

The mannequin women scratched and clawed at the shield to get at my daughter, but their long nails broke off with every blow. They screamed, "She is ours! She has always been ours."

In the shade of the shield, Naomi's resolve returned.

The mannequins backed away.

"I have to leave now, Dad, or I never will."

We eyed the door ahead, but Naomi could not get up, and I could not pick her up. I dragged her on my shield, covering her with hers. I fended off the mannequin attacks with my arms and body. They scratched and clawed at my new clothes, tearing my flesh in the process. I was covered in my own blood, but pain fueled my resolve to save my child. Even if it killed me, I was getting her out of there.

The mannequins crowded closer and closer until they surrounded us, leaving me no escape. My heart skipped several beats. Then, I remembered the angel had told me I must do without to go within.

"I have no strength, no weapon, no power. I cannot do this alone." I took Naomi's shield and reflected the great spotlight to fall on the advancing army of angry painted mannequins.

They shrieked and parted, flailing their arms and screaming obscenities. Their faces and arms began to melt in the intense heat from the light of my shield.

I placed one of Naomi's hands over her heart and the other over her eyes. She came back to life.

"Do what I do, sweetheart." I never thought I would ever get to say that again. "Don't think about the past or what lies ahead. Concentrate on the now."

A great light from the agate stone in her chest erupted to consume the light shining on her shield and reflected back an image to the mannequins.

They stood frozen, marveling at the true Naomi before them. Her genuine beauty became an intense heat that mesmerized them, and slowly they melted into the floor of the great hall, screeching, wailing, and cursing.

"Dad, we need to go now." Naomi reached up with both arms.

I pulled her up. "I've got you, Naomi."

"I can't do this without you."

"I am here, my daughter of the beautiful heart."

She couldn't get up. Her legs had lost all their strength. I picked her up and took one small step at a time, slipping and falling to my knees every few steps as the melting mannequins continued their attack, grabbing and scratching at Naomi as they disappeared into the floor. I chased away all thoughts of not reaching the exit and screamed, "I will not fail you this time!"

I lifted Naomi higher, away from the sea of stinking goo of melted mannequin mud that continuously flowed down the hill back the way we'd come. It was difficult for her to leave this place. It had become too dear to my daughter, and therefore deadly.

Naomi grasped at the pieces of mannequins with arms laced with all sorts of bracelets, hands adorned with rings on every finger, melted torsos dressed in the finest clothes, and beautifully styled hair with perfect makeup. She was still tempted to lose herself in this sinking, melting sea of lifeless false beauty.

"I still want it, Dad. It's been the only me I've known for so long."

I wanted to take the sword and spear of one angel and the bow and arrows of the other and kill them all. Then I remembered what my dad told me in his garden patch. "Don't be afraid, I believe in you."

I screamed with all my might at the mannequins tearing and grasping at my daughter. "Her name is Naomi. She is called Pleasantness. She is enough. She is perfect. I could have no better daughter than Naomi."

Immediately, the remaining parts of the mannequins burst into thousands of pieces, though they were still alive and grasping for Naomi. Their clothes melted, the jewelry released itself, and their hair disappeared in wisps of smoke. The last to go was their immaculate makeup, which streaked down their blank faces as they puddled on the ground.

Only the white melted goo of plastic figures with no faces, no purpose, and no names remained. Naomi screamed at the loss, believing she still needed more to be more. The more she cried and reached for the lifeless melting mannequins, the more she became like them. She jumped from my arms, frantically scooping up the mannequin goo and rubbing it on her arms.

I wrapped my arms around her waist. "No."

She turned to see her reflection in a tear hanging on the edge of my eyelid. "You do see me, Dad."

"I do, and this is not you."

She pulled back her arms and folded her hands on her chest where the agate beamed like the sun.

The mannequins disappeared into the stinking mud.

Naomi took her shield and covered her face from the temptation that could only lead to her inner death. "I'm ready, Dad. Let's leave this place now." Her face returned to its original beauty, and she walked from the great mannequin hall on her own. She wavered from exhaustion and started to faint.

I caught her in my arms just before she fell back into the goo, still writhing in the pain of losing Naomi.

I touched my chest where the agate stone resided and grabbed the two shields. My energy surged, and I raced from the great hall out onto a mountain ledge, where I gently laid Naomi on a patch of soft earth.

I ran my hands over my back and arms, then thighs and calves. They bled from the mannequins clawing and biting at Naomi. Strange, the wounds bled, and I ached all over, but the mannequins never touched me. My bleeding wounds were hideous.

The People's Protector passed over, waving the great sword. "Now you know the joy of taking the pain of defending Creator's own. Do not trouble yourself with the question any longer."

"What question?"

"What would have happened had you not been here? You were."

He left a trail of stars behind him like the Milky Way. One in particular sparkled brighter than all the rest.

The People's Protector turned and grinned. "That star is called Naomi. It will live forever, like her."

I sat beside Naomi, and we both fell asleep. For how long, I don't know.

I woke to a little sparrow on my shoulder flapping its wings and chirping.

So it is true that not a sparrow can fall to the ground without Creator knowing it.

I turned to my daughter beside me. Naomi slept peacefully.

My wounds were healed, but the scars remained. I could live with that.
A cup of wine and a piece of bread sat before me.
The Great Voice whispered, *"Eat and remember. Everything."*

Though my soul may be set in darkness,
It will rise in perfect light;
I have loved the stars too fondly,
To be fearful of the night.

—Sarah Williams

CHAPTER 60

The Second Ascent

Refusing to forgive is the doorway to death before its time.

—the author

I GAVE THANKS. As I savored the bread and wine, memories of all my wrongs I had forgiven myself for flooded my mind. I felt good. But those memories were quickly chased away by those I didn't want to forgive. "Who cares, anyway?"

"*I do.*" The Great Voice shook the ground with his pronouncement. Small soldiers of light with long whipping canes herded all the wrongs I had yet to forgive myself for, their numbers great like a herd of foul-smelling pigs. From every direction on the compass, they presented themselves before me like a military parade.

"What's this?"

The Great Voice boomed like a cannon. "*Make peace with this army, or you will be defeated.*"

"My wrongs were because of what they did to me. I never asked for them. I just wanted to be left alone. They should ask my forgiveness. They're the guilty ones. Who is it I must make peace with? Not them. They hurt me. They made my life miserable. I did what I did because of them. I only wish I had hurt them instead of my family—instead of Naomi."

"You speak your own answer."

I accepted the truth. "It's not about forgiving them, is it?"

The Great Voice remained silent.

Exhaustion overpowered the conversation. Finally, I surrendered. "Okay, who then? Who do I have to forgive?"

The Great Voice whispered in the soft sound of butterfly wings. *"You, for not having forgiven them sooner."*

As often as I look upon the cross,
so often will I forgive with all my heart.

—St. Faustina

CHAPTER 61
The Mercy Seat

Stop leaving and you will arrive. Stop searching and you will see.
Stop running away and you will be found.

—Lao Tzu

I FELL BACK, flat on the ground. "I can't do it. I've lived with these things too long. They are too much a part of me now. The horrible things they did to me gave me strength to help others, to be here to help Naomi. I can't. I just can't."

"*Rather, you won't. Correct?*"

"If I forgive myself for the things I did because of what they did to me, what will I have left?"

"*The answer to that question is the one you need most.*" The Great Voice hovered above me, and a great hand pointed to Naomi. "*She has forgiven, but she can't forgive if you refuse.*"

I glanced at Naomi, whose sleeping face bore a smile. Her light breathing was as peaceful as a cat purring.

"What do you mean?"

"*A refusal to forgive is a refusal to live. She cannot rise from her slumber until the entire world you forgive.*"

"But I'm not Your Son who gave Himself up for the entire Universe. He saved everyone."

"No one asked you to save anyone. You've only be asked to help save one, but in doing so you will save a small part of the Universe. It's My way with My people."

I got back on my feet at the sound of many men moving stones. The image of the Mercy Seat I'd seen in pictures was being built and carved by tiny men who all looked like me. Each had a word written on his shirt that described my best qualities, so many I'd forgotten were me. They quickly finished and scampered away like they were about to be consumed by a fire. The Mercy Seat I had constructed boiled red and black like a raging fire storm. As I walked around it, moving pictures on the panels on every side were all scenes of things done to me as a child, some terrible, some unthinkable. I swallowed hard.

"This won't be easy." I clenched my fists in a growing rage. My body shook like an ever-increasing earthquake. "See there. I told you. They did those things to me. I did nothing to them, and they plundered my soul until I had so little of me left that I hardly resembled who I was supposed to be."

"You have eaten of the bread and wine. Now you remember."

My face burned red hot. "But have I not forgiven them? Don't you believe me?"

"To a point. You were forgiven even when you asked insincerely. But you extended yourself mercy I never gave. This is your Mercy Seat, mercy extended to others but not to yourself. You built it for yourself out of the stones of what others did to wrong you. This Mercy Seat became your power—a false power. You built it in your own image."

"I did not."

"You would argue with Me, even still?"

Exasperated, I barked, "Yes. You are God. You're supposed to be able to take anything I dish out. All loving, all knowing, all powerful, all forgiving, right?" I couldn't believe I talked to Creator this way. I was losing myself in this conversation.

The Great Voice cleared His throat. *"Then I will be patient with you, for a time. Look at the top of the altar."*

All the evil and wrong things that I had allowed myself to do were piled high on the Mercy Seat of my own building, stacked on the stones that were the backs of those who wronged me. Their faces were carved in the stones, all grimacing at the burden they held up—my burden. I had designed and built a Mercy Seat for myself that entertained the joys of the Evil One. I had forgiven the wrongdoers but felt no need to forgive myself for the evil pleasures and thoughts I had allowed myself. The Mercy Seat I had built for myself was not of the Creator.

"I thought I was forgiven for all of that. I thought you took my sin away before I came to the Name Tree."

"*I did.*"

"Then what am I missing?"

"*That is the right question.*"

"What is the answer?"

"*There is but one thing left I require of you.*"

"What is that?"

"*Forgive yourself for the sinful things you learned to do because of the wrongs done to you by the hands of others.*"

"I can't."

A great wind blasted me to the ground. "*You will, or Naomi will go no farther.*"

"I can't take her the rest of the way."

"*Do not test me, son. Your way got you here, and now you want to try it your way again? Did visiting the Tree of Human Choice not teach you anything?*"

The beautiful fruit the Great Serpent had tempted me with was dangled in front of me. I wanted to take Fruit of Human Choice so I wouldn't have to confess my power, the It, was what had made me what I was.

A small, slimy voice whispered, "Told you I'd be back. I will never leave you nor forsake you." The snickering of a thousand demon voices rang in my ears like cymbals.

More fruit appeared, each more luscious and delicious looking than the one before, but with a worse sin I could not forgive myself for written on it. The demon voices grew louder with each new piece of fruit. I couldn't think straight.

The Great Voice barked, *"Silence!"*

The demons immediately stopped their chatter.

I shook my head, trying to regain my dulled senses.

The Great Voice chided me. *"Only you can dispose of these properly."*

Properly?

On the ground next to the Mercy Seat, two words were written in soft gray clay.

ουιλοΥω ολα

My anger flashed. "Why did you have to write it in Greek?"

"You were the scholar, remember, praised for your gifts and abilities. Because of the pride in your accomplishments you still enjoy, you must read it so."

Memories returned of the long hours spent studying Greek early mornings and late nights to make the perfect test scores I coveted in seminary. Then, I remembered the day I heard a small knock on the door of my study.

There stood four-year-old Naomi, dolls in hand, wanting me to play. I cringed at what I did next. I chased her away because I believed what I was doing was far more important than being with her.

A great weight settled on my shoulders. I was mashed to the ground.

I tried to recall the words and meaning of the Greek phrase before me. The longer it took me, the deeper I sank into a pit of mud made from the drainage of the cracked open sores the mannequins had inflicted upon me. I racked my brain and flailed my arms, but grasping for what, I didn't know.

I cried out, "I don't remember how to read the words. Please help me."

The words instantly were translated on the Mercy Seat. I read them aloud.

"Confess all."

It felt like a baseball bat had hit me squarely in the forehead. The weight fell from my shoulders, and the ground underneath me dried up. My wounds healed, and the desire for the fruit left me. I sat and found Naomi standing over me. She reached down and pulled me up.

The Great Voice spoke, *"She cannot if you will not."*

I realized then what I had to do. I recalled all the memories of things done to me by the hands of others. I then remembered all of the wrong things I had allowed myself to do because of their abuse—self-medication, self-protecting behaviors, anger, violence, abuse, hate.... I confessed all I had not forgiven myself for, the wrongs I had done because of what others had done to me.

"I forgive them all, and I forgive me." Though lighter, I still had a weight pulling me down.

Naomi took my hand. "That's only part of it, Dad."

Then, I called out all the hidden grudges, designs for revenge, the things I had refused to forgive because it gave me power over people.

I patted the dust from my clothes like a kid trying to keep his pants clean for Sunday school. Memories of the secret things I'd yet to forgive myself for floated away in the dust cloud. I breathed in fresh air that had the scent of a pine forest.

The Great Voice, in a pleasing tone, announced, *"The things done to you by the hands of others and things you did because of them, I declare forgiven."*

The sound of a great crowd approached, and Naomi quickly hid behind me. Each one walked stiffly, like stick people with signs in their hands. Everyone I had ever wronged stood before me, waiting for me to speak.

"I thought I was forgiven." I looked around for the Great Voice, but all I could see were dark boiling clouds swirling around us.

"Please help me."

The Great Voice declared from the churning thunderheads, *"These are those who learned by your hand to harm others."*

"Does this ever end?"

"Yes, my son."

"Then why is it so complicated?"

"You made it so," the Great Voice answered.

"But I made amends with all I could and now have forgiven myself. Was that not enough?"

"It was." The crowd turned slowly to walk away like a defeated sports team—all but one person who looked vaguely familiar.

"Then what must I do?"

A familiar snicker sounded. "She cannot forgive because I have not forgiven you. And I never will."

Naomi peeked around from behind me, "SHE!"

In the sweetest, sloppy, wet kiss of a voice imaginable, SHE coaxed Naomi. "Just come over here with me. We'll turn our backs on all the past so he can't hurt us anymore."

Naomi started toward SHE, but I held her close.

"Come to me, my baby. Let me cuddle you in my arms. We'll forget your father ever existed."

Naomi's eyes had glassed over. She tried to pull away.

I held her firm. "Touch your heart, Naomi, now."

The power SHE exerted over Naomi was far too strong for me but not for the light that could expose the truth. I grabbed Naomi's hand and placed it on her chest that glowed like a brilliantly illuminated agate.

Her eyes cleared instantly. Naomi looked back at SHE, whose folded arms now bore tattoos—"Unforgiven" on one and "Grudges" on the other. "Revenge" was written on her forehead.

Naomi said with strength of the People's Protector, "All is forgiven, all is forgotten." Naomi turned to SHE. "You made Dad the monster in you."

SHE shrieked like the demon that lived within her and flew away on the wings of a dragon.

I sniffled. "I forgave them a long time ago, Naomi. I even forgave her for not forgiving me. I don't understand."

Naomi became a little child clad in a bright summer sundress and white hat with multicolored ribbons dancing in the breeze. She pulled a glowing blue plastic Easter egg from the basket she held. "Open it, Dad. There's a very special surprise for you within."

One word was painted on the outside of the Easter egg. "Within."

There was that word again.

Then, I remembered Granny's words. "Be honest within yourself."

I twisted the blue plastic egg and opened it to see "Within." There was no candy or toy, just a small folded slip of paper that resembled a fortune cookie message. I remembered the Amazon-esque angels' words. "You must do without to go within."

I unfolded the paper and read out loud the two words written there. "Forgive yourself."

I looked at Naomi who had returned to her adult form.

"You can do this, Dad."

I shook my head, wanting to hide under a rock somewhere.

Naomi didn't blink. "If you don't, I can't."

I weakened for a moment. "But how can I forgive myself if they don't forgive me?"

The crowd turned around as if to claim victory.

I found myself as a child in a tiny church building where my uncle preached a Hell-fire and brimstone sermon so loudly it hurt my ears. He railed about how a person must make every wrong in his life right and beg forgiveness from those he had sinned against.

I shook my head in confusion. If I could right every wrong I'd ever done and make it up to the people I had wronged, then why did I need saving?

The preacher stopped in mid-sentence and pointed his finger at me. "I'm talking to you." Fire breathed from his nostrils as his teeth gnashed. As a newly baptized eleven-year-old, I had bought into the fear he so willingly forced upon me. I wanted to please God but even then was unsure how anybody could do that. From that moment on, I grew up believing no one could, especially not the ones who preached such garbage. But somehow that teaching had lodged in the deepest part of my soul.

The Great Voice spoke like a volcano erupting. *"Forgiveness never depended on the willingness of the wronged to forgive."*

My eyes burst open. I saw more clearly than ever before. "I can see."

"Yes, you can."

The crowd disappeared.

"I can forgive myself because forgiveness begins within."

Naomi took my hand. "I can, too, now."

"Freedom was never about the ones I'd wronged forgiving me, or me forgiving others. It was always about me forgiving me. The other naturally follows."

Naomi took my hand. "We can go now."

We can only tell the truth when we cease to identify
with the part of ourselves we think we have to protect.

—Ram Dass

CHAPTER 62

The Third Ascent

Forgiveness is setting the prisoner free,
only to find out that the prisoner was me.

—*Corrie Ten Boom*

THE ROCKY PATH we climbed became so slippery and difficult, we had to crawl on our hands and feet like when we worked our way up the steep hillside after we found the Name Tree the first time. Great boulders blocked our way, requiring Naomi to stand on my shoulders to gain the top and then pull me up. This was no easy task for either of us and risky at best. Finally, one large boulder stood between us and the top of Holy Hill. Two small hammers and chisels lay at our feet.

I shook my head. "What good are these? We'll be here for eternity trying to break this rock."

The Great Voice spoke from the rock blocking our path. "*You will indeed if you will it.*"

Naomi and I went to work on the boulder that grew larger with every chunk we broke off. With every strike, a new piece grew in its place, bearing the face of each person who had distracted Naomi from following Creator. We chipped harder and faster, but to no avail. The rock became larger and larger, towering over us to block out the light.

I screamed, "This is too much. If you would but let Naomi pass, I will gladly stay here forever. Just let her go. Please." I sat and cried, exhausted from all I had encountered since I'd crossed through the thin veil.

Naomi looked at me with surprise. "Dad?"

I looked up, wiping my eyes.

"For me? You would do that for me? Stay here forever if it meant I could go free?"

"Yes."

Naomi drew back her hammer back. With the force of ten thousand Amazons, she smashed the great boulder into a thousand smaller boulders. From the wreckage came deafening screams of all those who had blinded Naomi into believing she had to have their approval to give her purpose. Tiny mouths gaped open on the small boulders that rolled down the hill into the abyss far behind us, but no sound could be heard from there.

The Great Voice announced, *"You must turn your back on all those who you believed gave you identity."*

"I know who I am." Naomi turned her back on the small rolling boulders as the last one shrieked in pain and planted at her feet.

I took her hand. "We don't have far to go."

You are the place where God chose to dwell.

—Henri Nouwen

Who am I, except who I am in God?

—the author

CHAPTER 63

On Top of Holy Hill

The voices of a thousand spiritual guides sing but one simple song.

—the author

A DOOR NOT there before planted itself upon a garden-like tiled patio. It opened into a bright, inviting room walled with agates that mirrored our every move. It was as if they were alive and searching for a home. Every color imaginable sang its own song as it joined with the others in perfect harmony, then separated for a moment to share its own special tune while the others listened. It was like one note playing on a billion-stringed harp. Each individual note was as strong as all the others combined because it was unique. None tried to outdo the other as each took its turn to play its unique tune.

I looked at Naomi like it was my first time seeing her uniqueness, the true beauty of a translucent soul that surrounded the golden heart beating in her chest.

She stretched out both arms to receive the agates and invited them into her soul. She wrapped her arms around them all. I clearly heard each tune as the agates entered Naomi's soul.

The Great Voice declared, *"Blend together and become one. This is the purpose of the Universe."*

As my eyes adjusted to the wonderful display of lights that traveled deep within Naomi, I was startled to find countless faces of people sitting in the room with no walls in sight.

Naomi stepped forward. "Don't be afraid. They have always been with us, Dad."

Every spiritual guide of every belief throughout human history sat on a golden mat encircling us, their gazes fixed on Naomi. The multitude of the spiritual was endless. Some were the least likely people I'd ever expect to be in this crowd, some of whom I recognized, some of those I once thought I taught.

A homeless man was there. He used to pick wild flowers for old ladies who were shut in. The welfare mom who died in our home was there, too. She had shared all she had with mentally ill street people. And a prostitute, sat up front. She gave her earnings to buy medicine for those who couldn't afford it and food for hungry children in the projects.

I knew these people, but they weren't looking at me. Their gazes were fastened on Naomi. Their eyes suddenly closed in meditation. They had gathered for her.

Naomi wandered in and out of the crowd, touching each person as they contemplated the Universe. Each smiled as she passed.

How can they see Naomi with their eyes shut?

"Blind eyes are healed in this place," the Great Voice announced.

The crowd of spiritual guides instantly stood, and their eyes shifted to me like professors waiting for an answer to some deep theological question. In one voice, they asked me, "Can you finally see?"

I looked at Naomi. "Yes. Yes, I can."

The sound of large rocks falling, like a wall was being battered down, deafened my ears. The spiritual guides stood still, and in a loud voice, they cried in unison, "Walls were not created by the One Who Frees."

The room faded away into an endless green field with wildflowers of every kind. I looked around the meadow but could not find the Great Voice speaking through the multitude of spiritual guides who were all saying the same thing.

Out of the thousands of flowers, the Great Voice spoke. *"There is no need to search for me. I am the Always and the Everywhere."*

Naomi stepped forward as the swirls of agate beauty erupted in a myriad of songs from her heart.

In one voice, the spiritual guides called, "You must become all that you may become none."

Naomi whispered back, "That, I understand."

Suddenly, a towering tornado of blue flame erupted in a flash crossing the great green field of wildflowers toward us.

I felt no fear, and Naomi stood taller and stronger than ever before.

The blue flame tornado entered the spiritual guides as they sucked in a deep breath. Their eyes turned blue and projected beams into one ray that stopped short of Naomi's face.

She didn't move, but the look on her face said she was making a great decision—an eternal one.

"Now I know." The beams began humming a familiar tune as they filled her soul. As she listened to the blue ray song of light that refracted into all colors imaginable, she burst out laughing like she used to.

The Great Voice laughed like one who had just found the greatest treasure of all time. *"No tears shall be shed here,"*

I fell to my knees and cried with joy. I was so happy I couldn't speak.

With all the might of the Universe, the Great Voice shouted, *"Naomi, my daughter, has returned!"*

The great crowd of people who sat in the stadium surrounding us appeared in the green field of countless wildflowers. They began a chant that became louder and louder until I had to cover my ears.

Naomi grabbed my arm. "Dad, they know my name."

The crowd never stopped cheering, "Naomi, Naomi, child of Creator."

...since we are surrounded by such a great cloud of witnesses,
let us throw off everything that hinders...

—Hebrews 12:1, NIV

Truth is truth. If truth only comes from Creator,
then what does it matter who speaks it?

—the author

CHAPTER 64

Letting Go to Hold on Forever

The most important hour is always the present.
The most significant person is precisely the one sitting across from you
right now. The most necessary work is always love.

—Meister Eckhart

IN THE CENTER of the great green field with thousands of wildflowers, the Name Tree appeared in full bloom, covered in bright green leaves, ripened fruit, and flowers I'd never seen. We walked over and sat in its shade.

Naomi was completely restored. Her gown of translucent blue glowed in the brilliance of a sunlit sapphire. Suddenly, from everywhere, waves of rainbow butterflies surrounded us. They circled and landed on Naomi, then more came, covering her from head to toe until she wasn't visible anymore.

"They tickle, Dad." Naomi giggled like she did when she was but a little girl. She reached into her pocket and pulled out a stone on a sparkling gold chain. The stone was of the purest white. She held it up and smiled. "Isn't it beautiful, Dad?"

"Yes, Naomi, it is."

A great hand reached from the sky and wrote the letters of her name in gold on it.

Naomi placed the gold chain with her name rock around her neck.

The Great Voice whispered, *"Never forget that you are my child."*

Naomi spoke in sounds like the trickling stream that bubbled past the Name Tree. *"I won't, dear Creator."*

Something fell from the sky. It was white like coriander seed.

Naomi asked, "What is it?"

The Great Voice answered, *"That is the right question. Now, feed on my presence and be satisfied with the person I have made you to be."*

Naomi took a bite, then looked up into the sky. "This is so good. It tastes like honey graham crackers."

The Great Voice declared, *"Eat my manna, and you shall live."*

Naomi took another bite while clutching the stone on the chain around her neck.

The Great Voice announced, *"It is done."*

The rainbow butterflies disappeared into Naomi, then she became all the colors of a rainbow, bursting into a beam of blinding light like the sun exploding through the clouds after a great storm had just passed.

When her form returned, she gave a smile I had missed for so long. "You can go now, Dad. I know who I am. My name is Naomi. I am at home—with myself."

I held onto her and wouldn't let go.

She plucked three rainbow butterflies from her hair and set them carefully on my heart. Each had one word written on it—Faith, Hope, and Love.

"I give these to you, Dad. The Three will help you find your way home, so you can tell others who have lost their way."

"But I want to stay with you. I don't want to leave."

"I wish you could. But we cannot be together here until you return."

"Return? Return where? I'm dead. I'm on the other side of the thin veil. I'm here with you."

"I know what I'm supposed to do now, Dad."

"I know, I know, but please, let me stay just a little longer."

"Let me go, and I will return to you."

We leaned back on the Name Tree.

"Rest easy now, Dad. You need to rest." Naomi laid her palm upon my forehead, and I fell fast asleep.

What the caterpillar calls the end of the world
the master calls a butterfly.

—Richard Bach

PART FIFTEEN

The Awakening

---

*To the one who is victorious, I will give some of the hidden manna.
I will also give that person a white stone with a new name
written on it, known only to the one who receives it.*

—Revelation 2:17, NIV

CHAPTER 65

My Return

In peace I will both lie down and sleep,
for you alone, Lord, make me dwell in safety.

—*Psalm 4:8, NIV*

MY EYELIDS FLUTTERED, then I woke to find myself lying in a hospital bed with my wife at my side.

"How did I get here? I thought I died."

"You did. At least, they think you did. Your heart stopped beating for a moment."

"How did you know?"

"I know you better than you think I do."

I didn't have to ask. "I shouldn't be alive. How did you get to me so quickly?"

"I didn't. I met the paramedics here at the hospital."

I looked out the window at familiar city landmarks glistening in the late afternoon sun. I was in the hospital where I had often visited the sick and dying.

"You took the pills and the Scotch whiskey all right, but I had forgotten my phone at home. I saw you get on the highway as I turned down our street to our house. I saw your text and found your farewell letter on the kitchen table. I screamed, 'No way!' I tried calling, but you must've lost service by then. I didn't know what to do, so I called the rangers at the state park. With the map you left, they got to you not long after you had... well, had taken the pills and drank the whiskey. They found you with your back against that big tree you'd told me about not long ago. You know, the one with the three names carved into the bark. You had an empty pill bottle in one hand and a half bottle of whiskey in the other."

Wait a minute. Three names?

"Was I dead when they found me?"

"Yes, but they think it was only for a moment before they found you in that deep dark hollow where the tree stood. They revived you on the spot, then used ropes to pull the emergency stretcher up the hill. When they finally got you to the ambulance, they rushed you here. Thank God." She broke down and cried.

"What happened next?"

"One of the EMTs said when your eyes opened for a second as they pulled you up the side of the hill, the sun broke through the gray clouds and lit up the forest like a blinding spotlight had been turned on full blast."

"How long have I been here?"

"You've been in a coma for three days."

"What day is it?"

"Sunday."

"I should've known Creator would do it this way."

"Who do what?"

"I'll tell you about it later."

"Good because we have something, or rather someone, you need to see."

The doctor stepped into the room. "Well, look who is awake and doing well. The nurse came to get me as soon as you woke up." He checked all of my vital signs. "How are you feeling?"

"Pretty good for what I just went through."

"You're lucky. We pumped most of the pills and alcohol out of your system. There is no damage. Sit up for me."

I sat and swiveled so that my feet touched the floor.

The doctor smiled. "Good. Walk for me."

I felt a little faint but had no trouble moving about. "Am I good to go?"

"Your wife explained the situation, and I understand things better now. If you'll agree to see a psychiatrist until you're cleared, I'd be willing to release you into your wife's custody. How does that sound?"

"I can do that, and I will keep my promise."

"All right, you're free to go when you're ready. I want to see you again in a week."

I nodded and smiled at my wife.

She went to the door. "Be back in a minute."

Still weak and groggy, I stumbled to the closet for my clothes. As I put on my pants and shirt, it was like the first time I ever dressed. These felt new and clean. For a moment, they glowed.

A familiar voice whispered, "*I brought you these. Wear them well.*" In a flash, Granny wisped by, and her comfort covered me like a warm blanket. I moved to a chair to put on my shoes, ready to live life again.

My wife rolled my step-daughter into my room in a wheelchair. Both were grinning ear to ear.

My step-daughter held a small, wiggling bundle wrapped in a lilac-colored blanket. She leaned over and uncovered the face of the most beautiful child I'd seen since Naomi was born. "Meet Papaw."

I couldn't believe it. Our new granddaughter had arrived.

"When was she born?"

"Not long before you woke up." My wife gently lowered her into my arms.

As I uncovered the blanket from the baby's face, I couldn't help but razz my step-daughter. "It's about dang time you finally let the secret out of the vault, Mom. Bethia is a great name."

My wife laughed nervously. "How did you know her name?"

I shook my head, brow furrowed.

My step-daughter threw up her hands and said, "We told no one, Mom. We wanted it to be a surprise for everybody."

I looked at my wife. "You didn't know?"

She shook her head. "Not that Bethia was to be her name. But the EMTs said you had mentioned it when you were still unconscious. I didn't know what it meant."

Puzzled, I looked back at my step-daughter, then at my wife. "Honest, I didn't know until just now when I spoke it."

My wife took my hand and squeezed it. "There were three names carved in the gray bark on that tree where the EMTs found you. Naomi's from when you carved it there years ago, and two others freshly done, yours, and—"

"Bethia's?" I said.

"Yes."

"How could I have known? I was out."

My wife's jaw dropped when she realized I was wasn't making it up. No one said anything for a moment. She looked at me, at my step-daughter, then back at me. "And they found your old hunting knife on the ground beside you."

"How could that be? I lost that knife decades ago in another state. My dad made it for me when I was a kid."

"The EMTs said there were fresh whittlings on the ground all around you."

I had no explanation. *Creator?*

No one could say anything.

Little Bethia cooed her first, breaking the silence.

My step-daughter laughed. "Like you always said, Creator can do whatever he wants, when he wants. Right?"

I nodded and smiled.

My wife hugged me. "No matter, you're back with us now."

I whispered, "With Creator, anything's possible."

In the mirror behind them, Granny appeared, smiling, a small agate stone hanging on a gold chain around her neck.

Just then, our son-in-law walked into the room. "Glad you're back with us, Papaw." He took little Bethia from my arms and handed me a small box. "This came yesterday by FedEx from your mom. She wrote on the note that it once belonged to someone named Granny, but she had given the heirloom to Naomi some time back. Strange, she just received it in the mail two days ago—from Naomi. She said the mailman apologized for it being lost for so long. The postmark on the package was March 15."

The day Naomi took her life.

I wanted to cry.

My son-in-law gently took the top off the small box in my hand.

I carefully pulled out a thin gold chain with a tiny multicolored agate hanging from it. "Is it all right if I...?"

He nodded and held Bethia so I could reach her. I placed the dainty agate necklace around her neck.

Granny's image in the mirror disappeared.

I prayed a short blessing over our new granddaughter.

Our step-daughter whispered, "Thanks, Papaw."

"So, what does our new granddaughter's name mean?"

The beaming new mother said, "Worshipping Daughter."

How fitting.

"May I hold her again, just for a minute?"

My son-in-law lowered the cooing bundle into my arms. I couldn't take my eyes off Bethia's face. So content, yet so vibrant. So peaceful, yet so alive.

"It's so nice to meet you, Bethia."

She smiled and opened her eyelids for just a moment. All the colors of the rainbow sparkled like swirling agates in her eyes.

I pulled her close, placing her tiny cheek on mine. "There you are."

See! The winter is past; the rains are over and gone.
Flowers appear on the earth; the season of singing has come,
the cooing of doves is heard in our land.

—Song of Songs 2:11-12

Do you remember who you were
before the world told you who you shouldn't be?
She's still there. Go after her.

—Erica Layne

CHAPTER 66

Final Words

Anam Cara—Celtic for soul friend.

—Granny

I RETURNED HOME from the hospital to find a most delicious red apple sitting on my laptop.

My wife asked, "How'd that get there? I didn't buy any apples. They're not even in season."

Through the window where I write, new leaves and flowers of every color danced in the swirling beauty of an agate.

"Granny."

The fruit of the Tree of Life is always the right fruit to taste.

—the author

In the dark night of the soul, bright flows the river of God.

—St. John of the Cross

WHAT BEGAN AS a quest to save my daughter became my own salvation. Truly, she saved me. It often takes one dying to save another. I couldn't have understood that until the end.

As I finish penning our story, I can't help but glance at the gift my wife gave me on the second anniversary of Naomi's death—my favorite picture of me holding our granddaughter Bethia. Beside it, I have a photograph of eleven-year-old Naomi leaning against the Name Tree, her name carved into the smooth, gray bark. And yes, she's wearing the hot pink jacket and smiling.

I do not at all understand the mystery of grace—only that it meets us where we are but does not leave us where it finds us.

—Anne Lamott

I Saw You in a Leaf

I watched you waltz in a descending leaf today
Released by none other but the dancer's own hand
Resting on painted heart where your name is written
As startling green faded yellow, your pain has fled.

Stretched faint, my soul lay bare on sandy river bar
Incessant tears, my heart opened that you may enter
Searching breezy sky of noisy jay bird blue
Willows swaying gently to soft wind song of you.

I waited, I wondered, would you stop to visit?
I cried, I begged, caring not for why you left
I called for you aloud but you did not answer
"Just... please, return to me, if only for a moment!"

My wilted soul could only wail at distant heavens,
"O daughter of mine, where did you go?"
I searched clouds of a thousand shifting shapes
None found so beautiful, as could form your face.

Tiny voice whispered memories of familial love
Once cradled and caressed in a new father's arms
Our lives together would share no more tomorrow
From cottonwood above you touched my heart of sorrow.

It was then, I saw you in a leaf.

—the author,
penned on Naomi's first birthday after her passing.

Only in the darkness can you see the stars.

—Martin Luther King, Jr.

TWO YEARS AFTER Naomi's death, I sat before a driftwood fire on a sandbar in the middle of the Mississippi River, wishing for a sign. I asked the night sky to soothe my aching soul. From the west to the east, a greenish spectral trail the color of Naomi's human eyes when she was born flashed across the night until the shooting star found her place on earth. It was Naomi's thirty-fifth birthday.

Two days later, our daughter put little Bethia's feet in the rippling waves of the vast ocean at the beach. Her soul runs far deeper....

Be who God meant you to be and you will set the world on fire.

—St. Catherine of Sienna

God never deserts the soul, but abides there in bliss forever.

—Julian of Norwich

Two YEARS TO the day since Naomi left, I stumbled down the hill into the hollow where the Name Tree stands. I brought flowers. They weren't needed. A young and healthy beech tree had sprouted from the remains of the Name Tree that lightning had struck. This time, I shed no tears.

Earth has no sorrow that heaven cannot heal.

—Thomas Moore

CHAPTER 67
One Last Story, Then I'll Let You Go

Perhaps they are not the stars, but rather openings in Heaven
where the love of our dear ones pours through
and shines down upon us to let us know they are happy.

—Eskimo Legend

JUST A LITTLE over two years after Naomi's passing, I was blessed to reconnect with a former member of the inner-city church we planted so many years ago. She was as ecstatic as I was to renew the friendship. We talked about the good ole times at the church and how much she appreciated me helping her get off the streets and into the life Creator always wanted for her. I asked about her children. Her oldest daughter had been one of Naomi's best friends and spent the night at our house more times than I can count. I told her I was the one blessed by those experiences.

She talked about how she "got off that stuff" and became a nurse. Sometime after, she married the man of her dreams. Unexpectedly, she became pregnant at an age most women wouldn't think of having a child.

"Brother, you won't believe what happened. I was lying in the hospital recuperating, trying to figure out a name for this child. I had racked my brain for months but never could come up with one. I just knew the nurse was gonna walk in the door any minute, and I wasn't gonna have a name to give that baby. So, I asked the Lord to help me." She paused and sniffled. "In a flash, I had a vision of Naomi and my daughter skipping through our old church building, laughing and talking like they always did when they were young girls. I got to thinking about the love in that church where 'God don't see no color' and how much that love changed all of us. Then, a voice said, 'Naomi.' I thought about Naomi's sweet spirit and how she loved all the children at the church, no matter where they came from."

I knew what was coming next, but I couldn't believe it until she said it.

"So, I named my daughter after your Naomi because of her loving spirit."

I held back the tears and thanked her for that eternal kindness.

Then, she said, "You won't believe this. She's fourteen now and just like Naomi. Kind, loving, caring, and always wanting the best for everybody."

We talked a little more and then hung up. I cried until no more tears would flow. Naomi's spirit lives on in those whom she touched by Creator's hand reaching through her.

Piglet noticed that even though he had a very small heart,
it could hold a rather large amount of gratitude.

—A.A. Milne

Happiness is not found in the things you possess,
but in what you have the courage to release.

—Nathaniel Hawthorne

CHAPTER 68

Parting Reflections

I sat by the River of Life and tossed in a rock.
"What are those?" asked I.
"The ripples of your life," said Creator.
"Where are they going?"
"Where you send them."
"But I know not where they go."
"Choose wisely the pebbles that you cast."

—the author

———————————

What we do now echoes in eternity.

—Marcus Aurelius

———————————

Your heart and my heart are very, very old friends.

—Hafiz

Go and learn....
...the people who have been broken the most, are usually
the ones who go out of their way to put others back together.

—Bianca Sparacino

Are you tired? Worn out? Burned out on religion?
Come with me.
Get away with me and you'll recover your life. I'll show you how to
take a real rest. Walk with me and work with me—
watch how I do it.
Learn the unforced rhythms of grace.
I won't lay anything heavy or ill-fitting on you.
Keep company with me and you'll learn to live freely and lightly.

—Matthew 11:28-30, The Message

Everyone you meet is fighting a battle
you know nothing about. Be kind. Always.

—Robin Williams

We don't always know why people do what they do.
Be careful how you perceive, and judge.

—the author

Be teachable. You are not always right.

—Unknown

Envision beyond what the eyes can see.

—the author

AFTERWORD

Thank you for reading *The Name Tree.*

As you might imagine, given the sensitive nature of the material, I have changed or eliminated all names associated with this situation except for Naomi's. I felt she deserved the recognition.

I am not a perfect man. As you saw in the passages inside, I didn't always put my family first, and we all suffered for it. That's not to say I was entirely in the wrong every time and everyone else was blameless. No, there's plenty of blame to go around. You know what they say about hindsight...

But this isn't about blame. It's not about how we got to where we were. It's about getting past it all, which I am blessed to say I did. And I live every moment of every day counting those blessings. Naomi gave me my second chance. I'm not about to waste it.

As I said, I've done all I can to protect the identities and hearts of the people who have already been battered by this tragedy. Still, it wasn't enough. Nor was sharing our story so you, too, might find hope where you think there's none. I wanted—needed—to do more.

To that end, 100% of my earnings from the sale of this book will be donated to the 988 Suicide & Crisis Lifeline, a service that answered nearly 5 million contacts in its first year—2023. I also respectfully ask you to consider remembering them when budgeting your annual philanthropic gifts. If you would like to join me in donating to this charity, you may make your check payable to:

Vibrant Emotional Health

c/o Development Office

80 Pine Street, Floor 19

New York, NY 10005

For further questions, contact the Development Team at development@vibrant.org or call (212)614-6315.

And please, above all else, if you have (or someone you love has) suicidal thoughts, stop what you're doing and seek help IMMEDIATELY. Call or text 988, the National Suicide and Crisis Lifeline, or chat at 988lifeline.org

ACKNOWLEDGMENTS

Writing this book challenged and stretched my every core belief and heart string. More importantly, it led me to a deeper understanding of Creator's love and faithfulness. I struggled deciding who I wanted to read the first draft of this manuscript. Several emerged without my seeking them. Thanks go to Arkansas Hall of Fame author and Methodist lay minister, Dorothy Hatfield, for her kind counsel and developmental insights early in the process. You helped me keep the story straight. I'm deeply indebted to my dear friend and paranormal expert, Ruth Weeks, who helped me understand the world into which I journeyed and gave crucial otherworldly counsel as I lived this story with my daughter. You were the *paraclete* I needed on the journey. To my nephew, Daniel Wood, who had a personal, familial stake in the writing of this book, your insights were invaluable, encouraging, and most of all brought peace to my soul when I doubted if I should even publish this story. To my development editor, Staci Troilo, you have become my new best friend, not only in our shared craft and making this book publication worthy, but as fellow traveler who has the heart to listen and the soul to comfort.

To Casey and Amy Cowan, Staci Troilo, Lisa Lindsey, Barbara Clouse, Wanita Humphrey, and the entire crew at Roan & Weatherford Publishing Associates, without your love, support, and expertise, this work would not have been possible. Thank you. The Name Tree is our book.

And, most importantly, the greatest appreciation and much love goes to my wife, Lisa. You walked every step of this difficult path with me. You cried and you rejoiced with me throughout the grieving and writing process. You truly are a friend like no other, save Creator. I could not have done this without you.

And yes, had you not been there with me, Creator, I would still be in the abyss. You're the best friend a human being could ever have.

ABOUT THE AUTHOR

Anthony Wood lives with his wife, Lisa, at the foot of the Ozarks where he feeds the red cardinals, rabbits, and squirrels that visit his backyard. Anthony's historical fiction series, A Tale of Two Colors, is about his ancestor Lummy Tullos living through the troublesome decades surrounding the Civil War. Anthony's writing has won a number of awards, including a Will Rogers Medallion Award for one of his western short stories, and he was recently inducted into the Arkansas Writers' Hall of Fame. He is President of White County Creative Writers and a member of Turner's Battery, a Civil War living history group. When he's not writing, Wood roams mountains and rivers in solitude and researches ancestors and historical events in his free time. He also enjoys photographing nature and visiting historical sites and old cemeteries. He lives with his lovingly supportive wife who claims he's the weirdest person she's ever met. Wood's heart is completely captured by his beautiful two granddaughters and handsome new grandson.